SARA KUAN

Vinay Singh

AF519993

BlueRose ONE.com
Stories Matter

© Vinay Singh 2022

All rights reserved

All rights reserved by author. No part of this publication may be reproduced, stored in a retrieval system or transmitted in any form or by any means, electronic, mechanical, photocopying, recording or otherwise, without the prior permission of the author.

Although every precaution has been taken to verify the accuracy of the information contained herein, the author and publisher assume no responsibility for any errors or omissions. No liability is assumed for damages that may result from the use of information contained within.

First Published in September 2022

ISBN: 978-93-5668-345-7

BLUEROSE PUBLISHERS

www.BlueRoseONE.com

info@bluerosepublishers.com

+91 8882 898 898

Cover Design:

Muskan Sachdeva

Typographic Design:

Pooja Sharma

Distributed by: BlueRose, Amazon, Flipkart

Thanks for support extended by Dermajoint India

DERMAJOINT INDIA

DER-JOINT HEALTHCARE PRIVATE LIMITED

Acknowledgements

I am thankful to all my patients who have given inspiration to think about writing the story. I am thankful to BlueRose publishers

I am thankful to Mr Sanjay Sharma for constant support.

Contents

Chapter 1: 2007, Delhi 1

Chapter 2: Anatomy Dissection Hall, 1989. 22

Chapter 3: Ahmedabad 29

Chapter 4: 2018 October. 31

Chapter 5: The beginning 48

Chapter 6: Gaj Gamini 63

Chapter 7: WhatsApp call at 3.14 am 68

Chapter 8: Suicide by choice 78

Chapter 9: Birthday 84

Chapter 10: Chest Pain 91

Chapter 11: Jaipur trip 95

Chapter 12: 2016 Pseudo movie show 99

Chapter 13: G I P Mall 101

Chapter 14: Sara Kuan 108

Chapter 15: Curses on the Soul 111

Chapter 16: I am THAT I am 116

Chapter 1

2007, Delhi

The cycle rickshaw is cruising at the usual speed. The rickshaw puller, a poor fellow must have had his share of gifts by the Sun God, but a bigger fire in the belly made him pull humans despite all odds and some maneuvers like whipping face frequently with *gamchaa* - a thin but long cotton towel easily wrapped around the head or shoulder and drinking almost boiling water from a plastic water bottle.

The distance to be covered is less than one kilometer from my workplace – my clinic but in this scorching heat of Delhi in June 2007, I did not want to get drained out. I could take my car but to drive just less than one kilometer in a hot boiling car is never a cool option.

My ICICI Bank is situated at Netaji Subhash Place in Pitampura, an upscale district center in north Delhi and has declined my request for honoring tax challan, as the bank officer on the other side of help desk informed me that the facility is available in a nearby ICICI bank branch in Pitampura itself at TV Tower.

I sincerely wish that the Government starts user-friendly multiuser kiosks at many places where tax payments along with various useful things like bill payments, information regarding study courses in the city or state, train, bus, flight information, postal department issues etc. for the use of a common citizen, are made available.

A common civil code or something more appropriate is needed for the real development of our country, maybe someday few politicians will understand and apply the real meaning of democracy to ease the life of a common citizen.

It is a distant dream to have all these facilities in an air-cooled atmosphere, at least for citizens like me in Delhi. I am not complaining though I am sharing a democratically viable and useful idea.

It is 29th June 2007, my chartered accountant has sent me the challan to pay tax in the bank branch.

Online tax payment portals are yet to kick start in our country. Many people like me are getting roasted in the heat of Delhi with a heart which says go and contribute to the development of our nation and the circumstances are shrieking in other direction.

Many times I feel pity for the poor rickshaw pullers, be it heat, rain or cold, and God has given the people of Delhi all the seasons special effects in abundance, these men keep doing their work to earn bread for their families.

My heart cries out for them when I see affluent passengers alighting from such tricycles carrying bags representing brands whose clothes may cost six months earnings of the poor fellow and arguing with the rickshaw puller for five rupees.

"*Bhaiya kal hi to das rupay me aayi thi aaj bees kaise ho gaya?*"

Another passenger will take pride in supporting the previous one "Ye *to loot hai, theek theek laga lo, hum to roz hi aate hain*"

The poor fellow has no other option but to swear on his children and plead. After a few minutes of a dramatic win by 5 rupees the ecstatic uptown ladies vanish behind huge gates of independent houses or flats. This is a usual scene in Delhi.

I wonder why the same human species never want to argue and bargain for a tag of rupees three thousand five hundred or more nicely stuck on a piece of cloth termed as a top or similar things.

I am sure that someday a wave of social networking will take the uphill task to make us understand the real difference between actual labor and cheating if not harassing or being harassed.

Nevertheless, I am lost in these thoughts and suddenly, my cell phone rings.

Being a doctor, I generally take all calls, but this is my lunch hour and most of my patients know not to disturb me unless there is an emergency!

But wait I am a dermatologist. I took up this branch among all big branches as they were termed, to have the least possible disturbance.

I am looking at the number flashing on the screen of my cell phone, generally, I do not pick up at this hour and later ask my secretary to give a call to the person calling, as most of the calls are enquiries about my availability on a particular day and for appointments. I have a foolproof plan of avoiding my cell phone number printed on my letterhead to save me from all this.

There is something in the number flashing which compels me to answer, although the bank branch is in front of my eyes and there is a limited time available before the bank official will ask me to come the next working day, I pick up the call.

This call changed my life, at least I think so.

Hello, I say.

A sweet but low-volume female voice greets me. "Hello, *kya main Dr sahab se baat kar sakti hun?*"

"That's right you are speaking with the doctor, tell me how I can help you?"

Surprisingly, I am not irritated about the questions at this hour and when I have an important task with limited time when the summer was at its peak in giving Vit D and sunburns.

After breaking the previous year's record, the maximum temperature was asking for another medal this year.

To escape the hottest part of the day, most North Indians prefer not to venture out in dry, hot air called *loo* in hindi.

There is no other way to put up a protest with Mother Nature.

I am beating all these and taking this call, wondering if the caller is enjoying air cooled surroundings in her office or home, not knowing my sweaty sultry status. There is an unexplained calmness in my voice.

There was something peculiar in the voice, an innocent appeal, raw but amplified enough to the magnitude of making everything surrounding me silenced.

I was lost in that voice. It seemed as if I have been waiting for whole of my life to hear this voice and the cosmos had finally chosen this day and time to fulfill my desire.

I sincerely wished it not to be a promotional call.

"Doctor, I have a problem of warts, and my gynecologist has asked me to get rid of them through a dermatologist.

I want to know more about it and also if you can do the operation for me?" That came as a rude shock, the voice which mesmerized me, a never felt so before soothing feeling gave me a shock that she is a patient with a not so difficult but also a not so simple problem to get.

Now such patients with a pre-formed diagnosis are difficult to handle, as they themselves have gained some knowledge or their treating physician has given them a brief introduction enough to scare the hell out of the patient.

If we see today's scenario, it is more difficult to satisfy patients as they have done some *research* enough to argue about the disease and side effects of the treatment, courtesy Google search engine. Patients now open the pages on their smartphones and start talking as if they have done a doctorate in the disease or the medicine. Nevertheless, back in those times, this pain was not there.

"Sure, I will help you" and with this I get down from the rickshaw, pay the dues, start walking slowly towards the bank.

My concentration is only on the call, something is keeping me glued to the call and the caller, which is very unlikely of me. As a doctor I do not explain much over phone call and moreover I have a timeline waiting at the desk of the manager in the bank branch.

But I am not able to visualize anything other than this call.

"Tell me since how long you have been seeing the warts?" A usual query.

"It has been 2 months and they are growing rapidly; I am concerned. I went to a gynecologist for treatment, she gave me some medicines but the warts are increasing so I asked her, and she suggested seeing a skin specialist for treatment."

"Ok, how did you get these warts? I mean, are you married? Does your husband have any such warts?"

"No doctor, I am separated from my husband and the divorce proceedings are going on. It has been almost 2 years since we met."

Another jerk, warts, divorce............ oh God what is next with this voice?

This comes as a news to me but knowing the nature of warts I am not surprised; however, I am surprised at my curiosity about this particular caller as I want to know more.

Generally, such stories are common with most of the doctors, where people have either a true story or made up one only to satisfy questions.

Most of doctors including me never delve into the reasons, we treat, get paid and both the doctor and patient are happy in the end.

If the patient is not satisfied, there are vast options in our country to take second or third opinion from the same specialty, from different specialty for example a skin problem is discussed with an orthopedic surgeon or a gynecologist, funnier is when people discuss some homeopathy prescriptions with doctors who do not understand the homeopathy science and vice versa.

Anything and everything are possible in India.

Mostly home remedies or treatment suggested by a friend, relative or an acquaintance is followed religiously. If that fails, local Chemist *wala bhaiyaa* comes to the rescue. Still not satisfied then, Indians believe that the quack or family physician, depending upon the IQ level of the patient, is God and will treat their miseries.

There is another savior and that is an old prescription for a similar problem either of self or any other fellow good society person ready to help, which is believed to be golden words written in stone plaque as received by Joshua in ancient times.

A medicine which costs more than a few rupees per day seems to be a burden on society but a bottle of wine which is produced for less than the cost of a tablet but sold for many hundred times the cost of production is a necessity.

Also, it is very common to say about complete failure and incompetency of the previous clinician and to thrash doctors in our country at the drop of an eyelid, nobody cares to keep a healthy lifestyle, but it is always easy to term doctors as dacoits.

Great usage of democracy. I am not a social worker or a politician who has taken the responsibility to correct wrongs.

Returning to the conversation with this patient, I continued "Oh, I am so sorry to hear that. As such, the wart if it is contracted through close body touch, can crop up and start spreading when a patient has lower immunity, but only the patient must know in his or her heart the source of such an infection."

I was again surprised to have talked on phone in length, usually I do it in my chamber and to maintain doctor-patient secrecy I do not discuss things on the phone.

Also, it is not like me to discuss about any personal information of the patient, but my psyche is not in my hands as this call is progressing.

My mind and heart are at war, the mind shouting and the heart relenting to ask more personal questions from this unknown, unseen patient.

Very much unusual for my professional life.

But here I was discussing a personal or rather a contagious disease with an unseen patient on the phone.

"Why don't you come and consult me in my clinic, and we can decide the future course of treatment?"

She asked candidly "How much is your consultation fee and how much will the treatment cost to me?"

These are usual questions from most of the patients, but there was something different in this conversation which I wanted to keep alive, at least for now.

"My fee is eight hundred rupees, and the treatment cost will be decided during the consultation. You said you have genital warts, it depends upon the numbers, size etc."

"Do you know my clinic address?" something about this unknown patient kept me talking. Usually, I presume that all patients who call me have most of the details with them, or else they promptly ask for anything missing.

Many times, patients do ask for verbal prescriptions, which I politely decline.

"Yes Sir, I have your address, my husband was your patient once for genital herpes at your clinic. I also consulted you in 2005 for pimples so

I am aware of the same."

Now that statement came as no surprise to me. But I wanted to continue this conversation.

"Oh, I see, probably your husband gave you all the infections."

"No doctor it is not him." Came a cold reply. How could I forget?

She has informed me about their physical separation a few minutes back.

I felt like a lame duck.

And a long silence as if the question I put was wrong enough to prosecute me or the patient talking to me has been caught unknowingly.

I was wondering if this woman is undergoing a divorce proceeding, her husband took treatment for genital herpes, and all probability that he is a promiscuous person, probably had gone for another episode to gift his wife some infections and she is shielding him in good faith.

But then how a viral infection could appear on her at a body part where only intimate contacts can give or take an infection when she has had no physical contact with her husband?

As far as medical science is concerned, a close body to body contact is the most common reason for transfer of contagious infections and the incubation period i.e., the time duration between catching an infection and its manifestation can vary from few days to months and in some cases years of interval is seen. A failed marriage, long separation and no contact but getting a wart like diagnosis is confusing. Probably, there is a lot more to know before I make a diagnosis and conclusion to start treatment if the patient wants.

Permutation & combination does work in many places. Typical of an Indian wife, I thought.

"Then only you will be knowing in your heart as who gave you all this infection. By the way do you have any other problem, I am asking because you visited a gynecologist." I was inside the bank but that has nothing to do now.

My call continued. I knocked the door of branch manager & gestured that the call and my tax paying both are important, he allowed both. So I am talking at the bank manager's desk sitting in his office getting my work done for the betterment of my fellow countrymen by paying taxes. My mind was still with the conversation, something was telling me deep inside my heart that there was a connection.

"No sir I do not have any other medical problem at present.

But sir if there is any treatment with medicines, I would prefer to go for that." I slipped the challan to the bank manager again gesturing him about the call and requested for the needful which he acknowledged to my relief.

I came out of the manager's chamber to keep the conversation between a patient and me private so that professional secrecy is maintained.

I looked at a quite deserted corner and spoke. "I cannot say if you have actual warts or something else, but as you have described, it seems so. Some viral infections can be treated by medicines, many need lasers and some may require treatment for whole life."

I tried to speak in a low volume but a clear voice so that except the patient on the other side, no one else could hear me. "I do not want to scare you but also, I am not able to give any advice for your problem or course of management because I have not seen the same."

This patient was surely different as she had some knowledge about disease which I prayed no one should get infected with. Probably this was one reason I did not get an irritating feel to explain patients and clear their useless but common queries about any deficiency in food which can cause such and such skin disease.

"Yes, doctor I understand, and I will see you at the earliest. Thank you." *Click*. That sound informed me that the candid call was discontinued. Candid? Was it, may be from my side but the caller did not even wait for me to say Ok or something similar?

Maybe, she was just taking advice and taking a step-in doctor shopping ladder. But all these thoughts were discarded by the unison of my heart & mind which said that there is something unknown in that voice.

I could think of a *déjà vu* given my medical background and intuitive mindset. I was not able to brush aside all debates between routine patient enquiry calls and some strange pull towards the caller.

After putting down the phone in my pocket and finishing my work in the bank, I collected the counterfoil and started to walk outside to go to my clinic.

"Hello doctor, how are you doing?" A lady on the other side of table in the bank itself greeted me. I tried not to recognize her as I do with every patient of mine, this attitude is to save me from a free consultation. With a smile I thought I will escape but she stood up and asked me to take a seat. In a bank often a seat is offered to prospective wealthy clients or who are thought to be a scapegoat for various investment schemes and loans. Well, to the best of my knowledge, I do not fall into any of these categories.

My mind could narrow down to only one possibility, free consultation in the name of a cup of tea. But how she came to know about my thankless profession, unless I give free services was a dilemma.

In that catch-22 situation I did not have any other excuse but to be frank that I was getting late for my clinic, but the lady insisted and spoke in a perfectly audible voice "Doctor you are very kind and knowledgeable, you treated my son 2 years back; he was suffering from atopic eczema and thank God, we found you. You treated him with easy medicines, and he is doing fine till date."

Mixed feelings cropped up in my mind. As I was getting free of cost word of mouth publicity, it felt good to the extent that I took the seat hoping it not to be an opening for free advice. And I was surprised at the memory of this lady. Probably being in the bank played the key for her to memorize important people and events.

"Oh, thank you so much for the kind words. That is mine and every doctor's job." Came my usual reply in such situations.

"No doctor he was taking treatment from many years before, but there was no relief, it had made our lives very hard & disturbing before you treated him."

"What is the name of your son." I interrupted before she could start a series of cursing my fellow fraternity countrymen, known as doctors.

This is a common finding in our country's morning walk, kitty, same job etc. groups. Having asked the name of the child, a flash of thought crossed my mind. I did not ask the name of the caller with whom I was talking for nearly seven minutes courtesy of my brain and heart who behaved like siblings fighting over an issue which is never there.

Oh crap! But still, I have her number in my received call list, after that phone call I have not received any call, so I had the liberty and ease of saving the same.

I was now engrossed to gather a name of the caller, should I call her again, no said my inner self. True caller came into fashion much later than the tax paying for that year. I could always ask my secretary to do the job of knowing the name.

I was updated by the caller herself about her marital and medical condition, and that she and her husband were my patients, a few minutes back and having received a good reputation from a bank employee who had offered me a seat just now my mind raced and reached a conclusion that I must save the number in a name given by me, unbiased by religion and refuted the idea of staff verification of her name. I thought for some names and remembered a Bollywood movie which I saw over the weekend along with my wife on TV while having dinner where the hero gives name to an unknown female in his life and saved the number as *Anamika*.

After having a few minutes of quick dispenser-made chai and thankyous I rush outside to find the Sun God in full throttle waiting to bake me.

I waited for another cycle rickshaw, surprisingly few minutes back I was at the same place outside the bank, talking to Anamika and I never felt the heat. I looked at the sky, begging for a smooth ride back and I reached my clinic in 15 minutes, completely engrossed in my thoughts about the case which she has discussed and of course drenched in sweat, parched without a proper name.

My secretary informed me that there are 3 patients I must see before catching a flight to Mumbai for a meeting scheduled for the next day. I was back to my own usual self-doing work.

6.00 p.m.

Indira Gandhi International Airport

I am walking towards the entry gate no 3 with my black stroller bag. For flights, I prefer to wear jeans and T shirt with sports shoes. Inside the airport terminal, after collecting my boarding pass for Jet Airways flight 9W 376 I find that the flight is delayed by 30 minutes. I roam around the terminal premises to look for something new, finding everything expensive I turn my gaze to people around me.

My cell phone ring startles me. *Anamika calling* is flashing on the screen. I felt to have skipped a beat or two.

I had forgotten the day's proceedings after I reached to the clinic and now before flying, I am receiving the call from a patient, from Anamika!

Usual practice of my reaction is not to attend but to send a text message about being out of station and a request to contact my staff for any information.

This helps save my emotions of not being in front of patients and it saves my time too when some patient unknowingly starts detailing about disease

not pertaining to my specialty or about a known relative suffering in some distant town.

My message to the patient saves my roaming talk-time too.

But here I press the accept call button. Slowly but steadily, I take the phone near to my ear.

"Hello."

"Hello doctor, I am sorry to have called you at this hour, but I wanted to know if you are available at the clinic so that I can consult you."

"No miss, it is OK for the call and incidentally I am flying out for a meeting, and I will be available next only after 3 days."

The online consultation was not in any distant dream of mankind at that era before Covid 19 hit our globe. If my flight was not delayed, I was not supposed to get connected to this call!!!

"Oh, I thought of getting it checked. You know sir I am in great tension." Tensions do not crop up so sudden is all which I can laugh off.

But I keep my thoughts private.

She continued "The gynecologist also has advised some vaccine to be taken to prevent cancer of uterus. And, she also has asked me to go for some test to detect if I already have developed something or not."

Cancer is one of the scary words in medical terms which if used at wrong place in society and wrong time can kill the patient even if there is none.

My sympathy towards this poor fated woman became more empathic, and I tried to console her.

"Look, first before any diagnosis, you should not start worrying. And cancers do not develop in young individuals so soon. Relax, I am sure you are not on any recreational drugs, alcohol & medicines like marijuana or dope."

"No sir, not at all. I am a pure vegetarian. Although my ex-husband has made me eat chicken and eggs sometime back, but I have left it now."

So, does that mean eating meat, eggs etc. make you stand in line with drug abusers, alcoholics and peddlers? Again, my thoughts got wrapped up into clutches of my grey cells which acted like doors of impervious metal.

My mind screamed, idiot she is in tension, probably in depression. Think about her marital discord and the medical fears instilled in her mind as if she has committed a crime and will be punished to get executed in an electric chair.

Be reasonable with her. She is a patient. I keep walking towards the boarding gate no 27 as there is still time and finding lots of empty chairs, I start talking comfortably to my patient about her apprehensions for getting cancer, vaccines, tests etc.

"Your problem may be minuscule but if you keep thinking about the same it will become a *mansik tanav,* take my advice either wait for a couple of days before you consult with me or see another dermatologist. There are many female dermatologists in Delhi, and I can refer you to them."

"No doctor I will wait for 3 days but will not visit another doctor as it is an embarrassing problem also, I have immense faith in you since I know you have treated me and my husband earlier."

I find that it is just 5 minutes left when the boarding gates should have closed for the flight to takeoff and the monitor near the gate is showing next boarding for AI 126, New Delhi to Hyderabad, delayed by 3 hours. Continuing my preaching on phone I checked my boarding pass only to find that the Jet airways flight is departing from gate 29 in the next 5 minutes.

"Listen miss I have to cut down this call as I may miss my flight. Take care we will get in touch soon. Bye." While disconnecting the call, I gathered my sole luggage and myself and dashed towards gate 29, fortunately it is next to gate 27 and in less than 20 seconds I am standing there with my breathing at a rapid pace.

The ground staff, before looking at my boarding card announced my name and inform me that I am the only passenger left in this fully packed flight.

I look at him apologetically, but he was kind enough to ask me to relax while he connected with the crew on the intercom to inform them that the last passenger has arrived at the gate, and he was checking me in. He swipes my boarding pass and lets me in, then is my turn to start running again, the way from gate to aircraft through the aerobridge suddenly seems very lengthy.

On the way 3 more ground staff confirm me by my name and ask me to hurry. At the aircraft entrance, the air hostess is all smiles as always and makes me comfortable.

She says that I have made it in a fraction of second otherwise she was given instruction by the commander of the plane to close and arm all the doors.

Do I get a gold medal or appreciation for sneaking into the flight in last of seconds left before officially it took off. I have been at the airport terminal for a very long time, comfortable enough for easily boarding the plane.

But I was busy on the phone talking to an unseen patient, about an unseen contagious disease which probably has been contracted through an infected partner and not her separated-under-divorce-proceeding husband.

Still, I could catch the flight. I feel better than PT Usha and same time irritated about the call.

I thank GMR for revamping the airport otherwise if I had to take the bus route, I would have missed the flight from the boarding gate to the aircraft. I sit on the only empty seat 1C, my favorite and clasp my seat belts.

The cabin crew was courteous enough to settle my luggage in the overhead bin.

In the meantime, captain has given final instructions and abiding to the same, the cabin crew has secured all the doors, and the aircraft starts moving out of the taxi area. I am able to control my fast breath owing to the sudden rush of adrenalin and sprint.

The cabin crew starts demonstrating the safety features, I feel a buzz in my jeans pocket. I look at a familiar name flashing, *Anamika calling*!

I take permission by gesturing as an important call from the cabin supervisor, who is busy demonstrating the safety features in English by now.

She allows for a short call, probably thinking it to be a call from my wife as I entered the plane, dashing and sweating.

"Hello. I am in the flight and cannot speak much. Please be very short" I snap.

"Hello sir, I just wanted to know if you have safely reached inside your plane or not because you were in a tensed mood when you were talking to me."

"Yes, I could make it in time." I am surprisingly calm with this lady. "I am sure that you wanted me to miss this flight so that you could come for a consultation tomorrow."

A great author has said that annoyance makes people defend the indefensible.

"No doctor, I would never want you to miss any of your work because of my misfortune."

I get a tap on my shoulder which I discover to have come from the crew member requesting me to cut the call.

"I have to stop talking on the phone or else they will throw me out, I am joking. My staff will inform you when I reach back. Ok. Bye & take care." "Ok doctor, I wish you safe journey back home. See you" *Click*

I put the phone on airplane mode and close my eyes.

The drama in my life from afternoon till a few seconds before unfolded and started flashing like a movie scene.

Never ever has happened in my life that I have attended a call in my leisure hours and that too for more than few seconds. Unprecedented has been for me to take details of an unseen, unknown patient. Strange of the patient to have called me again twice, once in the terminal and now in the aircraft. Does she have a family? Or maybe not. Or maybe there is something else.

I feel the need to quench my thirst, more so because of a fast run to be seated comfortably in the elongated metallic capsule along with 167 other human beings.

I press the call button for crew and as the plane has not yet reached the main runway, a crew member appears.

"Yes Sir, how can I help you?" says the lady smiling.

She seems to be from the northeastern part of India and her name badge says Linda.

"Ya, I need some water."

Most of the crew members have been trained to carry small water bottles to attend the call.

And so, she produces a bottle from her pocket.

"Thank you, Linda." She leaves smiling as usual before giving another bottle to my co passenger.

The name strokes my mind. My heart screams, 'idiot you did not ask the patient her name.

You have talked to her three times today, but you lost mind do not know the real name. A smile comes on my lips at the confused attribute of myself. Consolation is that I have her number and a pseudo name Anamika, maybe it could turn out to be the real one.

At least that is what I wished for before putting an eye shield to get some rest. My mind keeps on doing all sorts of permutations and combinations about the mysterious caller whom I have never seen, whose name I do not know. My brain supported my ego, but my heart still wished to hear the voice again, to meet *again*.

Chapter 2

Anatomy Dissection Hall, 1989.

R.N.T. Medical College Udaipur, Rajasthan.

There are 97 students in 1988 batch of M.B; B.S. in this college this year. Also, this year marks the 1st ever batch of All India Pre Medical & Pre-Dental Examination entry into various medical colleges of our country.

I am one of the All-India exam students as it was called, who joined this college to learn medicine in a city called Venice of India.

After having a strike of more than 44 days by a group called RMCTA (Rajasthan Medical College Teachers Association) our studies kick started and ragging or so-called *parade* on the campus came to a slower pace.

I am allotted 8th dissection table with 9 other students according to our roll numbers.

Till now I have not purchased any of the textbooks and I am in the same league as other hostelers are because of the ragging, the strike and a tough time coping without the comfort of parents.

We hostlers do not venture out much in the city, for the fear of being caught by seniors and falling prey to ragging again. But ragging has started giving us the confidence to pull on your life in difficult times and it has taught us to make friends in not so good times.

We freshers wear all white clothes, trimmed military cut hairline and black shoes, to be easily identified as freshers. The only thing that makes all freshers proud as medical students is our doctor's coat.

In the dissection hall, it is a nightmare to learn that some of the fortunate students who escaped ragging, including girls and day scholars have finished dissecting almost 40% of the cadaver (dead bodies either unclaimed or donated for studies).

Here, I am who does not know the difference between facia and skin, muscle, and tendon etc. ready to dissect the remains of an unknown human being's body partially immortalized in formalin.

Coming from a humble background of a non-English speaking school in Jhansi, I used to take *median* as a printing mistake in the book which many of my co-student colleagues have, called B D Chaurasia and used to read the same as *medial* for a good long time.

There is a bald associate professor Jhala Sir, who tries to keep himself awake during lectures in anatomy by our madam professor, who has a habit of winking at all important points.

The anatomy hall is noisy with the stink of formalin sailing from one corner to another. Medical students are comfortable with that smell, they have to get their bodies accustomed for the rest of their lives. It is different from that of a typical hospital smell but is closer to the same with a harder punch.

Students learn to dissect human bodies procured from mortuary after no one has laid claim for them or sometimes a donated body reaches the dissection table.

With dissection flows jokes, stories, eye contacts, and skipping of heartbeats when a good-looking person looks at you, many sparks of silent and obvious romance tuning into actual love affairs.

Overall, the dissection hall is an integral part of medical students' life where for 90 minutes you are free to shape your future life and, in some cases life partner too. Eighteen years or so is the ripe age for this venture when one feels that life is now set for a long path not to be traded alone.

Few cadavers harvest maggots. Jhala Sir religiously takes pain in re-treating such cadavers to be used by medical students. So many funny events happened daily on each of ten dissection tables. One such scandal happened at our table.

Imagine the corpses or cadavers lying overnight on table covered with a dirty cloth.

One fine afternoon our class entered to dissect the shrunken, dark partially dissected bodies.

We were at our table surrounding the cadaver, one side of the same was occupied by all boys while girls rested on the stools on the other side, giggling and speaking to each other in hush-hush voices.

Jhala sir was as usual half asleep. No other teacher had joined him. Boys visited our table from other tables, some to see the progress of dissection, many to be near to the girls of our table, and a few to visit their roommates. Each student in the dissection hall has to wear a long doctor's coat. Students wear stethoscope hanging around their neck, which is a very expensive piece of jewelry because it is boasted off to the general public with lots of pride in the heart of the person wearing it and the amount of hard work, struggle, teary emotions and time of youth life is spent to earn it.

It was almost half time for the class when one girl belonging to our table shrieked out loud.

All eyes and ears were directed automatically in her direction, one reason was her loud cry, another that she was the most appealing face not only on our table but in our class too. Her hand came out of the pocket of a long doctor coat, and she was seen holding a small piece of body of the cadaver, on a closer look it was the manhood of the dead person lying in front of us. She threw the dismembered body part onto the cadaver and ran out to wash her hands.

Most of the boys burst out in laughter. The girl was in tears and always sleeping Jhala sir got a shock of his life, took time to understand the situation before dismissing the whole class.

In Anatomy, to remember the origin and insertion of tendons, all foramen from where various nerves and blood vessels pass is a mammoth task.

All students hate it as it has less relevance in later clinical practice. Truly speaking I never understood the concept of anatomy but passed the exam with the help of senior's notes and guidance about the most important questions, thanks to the ragging earlier.

So, my career started in a different note. I always wanted to become a doctor. My father an engineer, never got recognition and salutations from the public in Jhansi as compared to few doctors, I knew at that time whom *sabziwala*, *chaiwala*, watchman, along with most educated people used to address with respect and recognize as *dactar saheb*.

I still do not understand why physiology and biochemistry are taught to us in the manner it is taught. Ragging, long strike and lost vision about the coming days were very confusing.

I had a plan to drop M.B; B.S. and do some other course. Also, living in hostel was initially very difficult. I was never a pampered child but in a middle-class family few comforts were there, which looked like seven-star comforts if made available in the hostel.

My father was firm about staying in the hostel, having spent his hostel life in IIT Roorkee, he gave me fatherly suggestion to remain in hostel so that I could become independent for any situation.

Today I can say he was right. I started taking my own decisions from then and I am doing it the same way. Though failures come in your path of *ekla chalo re*, I am now used to it. And happy.

I have travelled some larger parts of our vast country, all alone during most days of my college vacations. After having scaled a new part, I used to reach home in last 3-4 days when my father would proudly ask me about parts of the country I visited this time.

Since childhood, courtesy Hindi Bollywood movies from 60s to 90s where they inculcate the concept that God has made someone for you, the right time will come, and you will identify your partner just by looking into her eyes.

This was not an imaginary concept. For me defying gravity, usual social customs and beliefs has been part of my life.

My search for such a partner continued during my whole graduation. All in vain.

For post-graduation my fate took me to Jaipur, where I got stuck with Radiodiagnosis or the study of medicine and diseases with the help of radiations like X rays,

CT scans, MRI scans and Ultrasonography. I found it to be a non-clinical subject where direct patient interaction is lacking.

We learnt reporting X ray and other films without knowing the patient in air-conditioned rooms.

On rounds it gave pain to me to see our hard worked reporting not even being glanced by the clinician taking rounds. He or she will pick up a film and looking through the same give instructions to juniors to modify the treatment.

One fine day a friend from the city asked me for some treatment and doses for malaria. The world turned upside down because in the past 6 months of my radiodiagnosis training, almost no clinical interaction with patients, I had to excuse myself as my grey cells could not recollect the trade names of medicines. Was I wasting my time becoming a super technician who did not remember any disease and medicines? It was time to introspect.

I started feeling out of place in this branch of medicine. Could I surrender to being entrapped and not happy for the whole of my professional and personal life?

My mind and heart started revolting against my decision of joining this branch. But I was not in a position to say goodbye and settle for being a family physician with only M.B; B.S. next to my name.

Being the first medical doctor in my family tree has some weightage, compromises cannot knock on the doors of my life.

Having decided to give life another chance, I wrote the entrance exam again risking my career at Jaipur, against the wishes and advice of my friends, family and known acquaintances.

Only my consciousness was with me because I have an attribute- I never quit.

The risk was worth taking for as I got the branch of liking, my good fate was smiling and shining when I joined N H L Municipal Medical College, Ahmedabad in a subject where I could actually see many diseases with the naked eye, sometimes under microscope and the subject where use of Latin, Spanish and English languages give people jitters.

I am not a nerd, but I love dermatology, another exciting field is psychiatry. I had a reservation about shaping my career in psychiatry because coming from a tier C city and a humble lower middle-class background, I never wanted to be called as *pagalon ka doctor*.

Dermatology is my love second only to the soul mate I have been searching for. Having found dermatology, I was confident of finding the unfound one, some day.

Chapter 3
Ahmedabad

20th July 1996

After alighting the 2 x 2 video coach from Udaipur to Ahmedabad, with my luggage dumped on the road near Kalupur railway station, I find myself looking for an autorickshaw to go to the designated medical college.

The city is bustling with all sorts of means of travel from bullock carts to cars, red buses under Ahmedabad Municipal corporation and lots of dust.

I have to make it to the office of the Director of Seth K. M School of Post Graduate Medical Sciences, N.H.L. Municipal Medical College, Ellisbridge, before 12.30 noon as instructed by one Bhaya bhai telephonically.

He helped guide me the routes etc. to the office. I have a letter from the Ministry of Health Govt of India, stating that I have been allotted a seat for M.D. course for 3 years at Smt. Sharda Ben Chimanlal Lal bhai Municipal Hospital which is a wing of N.H.L. Municipal Medical College.

I found Bhaya Bhai, behind a small desk and files partially covering his smiling face, he greeted me and welcomed to the institute. After filling up forms I was informed to give joining at Smt Shardaben Chimanlal Lal bhai Municipal Hospital at

Saraspur near Kalupur railway station. In Ahmedabad Municipal Corporation (AMC), hospitals are scattered in old city to cater the population, and for the benefit of general public, there is a coordination between all 5 municipal hospitals, their working staff reports to the commissioner of AMC. There are corporators of respective areas who look after daily working and standing committee for each hospital which includes public representatives who work with the superintendents of different hospitals.

All the hospitals have been converted into teaching hospitals to overcome the shortage of working force. Undergraduate and post graduate medical students work as task force.

Nursing college under Gujarat University also uses these hospitals to train nurses. The work culture is very smooth and with minimal conflicts.

There are no differences within the unit heads of a particular department. No conflicts between different departments.

People work in unison and the students get a good environment to learn.

Chapter 4

2018 October.

It has been a long 2 years since we have talked. Although I have tried my level best to pacify the unknown tension between us, many times. I have tried to call from different numbers, as she never picks mine. I keep in touch by calling from different numbers, she recognizes my voice, which she is a fan of, and disconnects the call.

Be it Deepawali, Holi, her birthday or any occasion I keep in touch, informing her that she is always in my thoughts, no matter what ever has happened on that day 22nd June 2016 at 2.40 after noon in broad daylight.

She asked me to get her out of her mom's home and settle her at some other place immediately. We were sitting in car near Haldiram's at Crowne Plaza Rohini. She said that if I did not do it now, she will either cut off all ties with me or will cut her wrist.

I tried to pacify her in between her sobs but failed miserably.

She suddenly alighted from the car and started walking towards auto rickshaw stand. I knew that she is adamant.

Some days I have waited on the lane she used to walk to catch a conveyance at the particular spot in the vicinity of her home, hoping to catch her and ask the reason for her indifference.

All in vain. She probably has changed her route too. How can a person who loves you without any expectation, knowing that the Cosmos has made 2 souls for each other, the souls which get solace just by looking into each other's eyes even from a distance, be distant and not in talking terms anymore?

There has to be something else. She has never introduced me to her family in the past 13 years of personally knowing me.

Yet she knows that she is always there with me. I know that she loves me a lot. Today is 3rd Oct 2018, I receive a missed call alert on my mobile.

Missed call as I was airborne returning from a closed group meeting in Mumbai.

As soon as the flight touched down, my cell phone got the lease of life in form of signals from service provider in home circle. There are 4 missed call alerts. I am surprised as I am looking at her name along with my reception, driver and my wife's numbers. In the meantime, the aircraft is yet to taxi and almost all passengers barring me and a few old ones waiting for wheelchair, are in such a hurry as if the Pilot will take them to another city if they do not jump out or as if their respective houses are on fire and they have to rush to douse the same.

People who were sitting, enjoying food, games or movies on phone and other devices, who were sleeping or reading comfortably, now are rushing and pushing each other as the plane is going to blast.

Keep sitting on my seat 1C, I am glued to my phone screen, not watching anything else than the SMS alert for missed call bearing her name, wondering why she has called.

'Hi, I missed your call as I was traveling.

Please call my clinic staff and I will be in touch with you soon.'

This is the conventional message which everyone receives when I am travelling when they call.

She also must have received the same. So, she knows I was travelling. I tell my wife that I have safely landed and will be going to clinic from the airport.

She seems relieved and asks me to take proper lunch and not to overstretch my working hours. I agree for all her advice, a married man does not have many choices, but I know her devotion to me, and I love her for the same.

An arranged marriage but no kids after 10 years of marriage has made me a work alcoholic. The problem of not having kids has root cause in me, we are thinking of adopting children but have not decided yet. She works as a pediatrician, gets in touch with age groups ranging from day one of life to sixteen years and satisfies her need of caring and loving kids.

In a government hospital you get to see many patients and job satisfaction as well, she is getting both and is happy with her work.

Our working hours are such that she can take care of the home after five in the evening, while I do morning and evening shifts in the private clinic.

Next, I call my receptionist, informing that I will be reaching in an hour by 11.30 am and that she should arrange lunch for me.

She informs that ma'am (my wife) has already given her the same instructions.

"Any other calls?"

"Yes Sir, a patient who has consulted you some months earlier wants to talk to you, your phone was not reachable, and I told her that you are in flight."

She is talking about HER! I am relieved that she has got the message for my travel otherwise she could have thought worse, maybe I am thinking too much, biased.

In low-cost airlines with no business class having seat in 1st row has lots of advantages, although it comes after a not so nominal fee. As soon as the crew gave a green signal, I collected my small trolley bag and climbed down the stairs looking for proper network. At airport, network for cell phones is weak in the plane taxi area also networking with other passengers is not possible until you have known someone for some time.

Everyone is in a hurry.

My cell phone rang, and the call was from my driver enquiring about my arrival and the gate number where he was waiting for me. This indicated that cell networks are working perfectly.

Moving out of the red-colored gate number 2 I placed my cell phone in front of my eyes. Opened the call option dial pad, punched 5, and there she was.

Her number is there first as I type 5, this is to facilitate me, so I do not have to type letters, I do this for frequently dialed numbers.

"Hello, how are you?" I asked.

"I am fine. How do you think I should be after so much?" came a weak reply.

There was an obvious shakiness in her voice. Having known her closely,

I could sense that everything was not good at her end. Changing the topic seemed appropriate for now.

"I saw your missed call. Actually, I was in an aero plane, so the phone was not reachable."

"I know, your secretary told me. I called at the clinic when the computer aunty on your number started speaking about non availability of your cell phone."

"I see someone has been searching for me after a long time. I hope things are in order."

"Yes and no." was a short answer but I could catch the same disturbed voice.

"Why 'no'? And what 'no'?" I became concerned.

Silence.

"Did you get married? You had a plan to do so in October 2017."

"My time for marriage will be there from December 2018 till March 2019.

Will see if I get a suitable match."

"I thought girls when get married they severe their contacts. You never answered my calls.

I tried my best in the past 2 years."

"Are you complaining? I am not in the mood to argue.

Please, it has been the worst part of my life."

"Hmm.... without me ....it had to be." I mumbled loudly.

"Yes, without you, and your support.

A lot of bad things have happened in my life; I do not want to relive that phase again."

"I am always with you, always at the same place.

Ok bad dreams are not to be remembered. I am going to the clinic.

I would like to meet you in person. Can you come?" I said.

"Maybe, I cannot say."

"Why? What is going to hold you? A lot must have happened, share with me.

I know you want to tell me everything. So come over, we will talk." My eagerness to know all was evident.

"Are you sure that you want to meet me?"

"Of course. I have been waiting for this day."

"*Pata nahi*, you may not find me appealing as earlier." She spoke in a low tone. A sense of dejection was in air.

'Why are you saying so? You know, I will be delighted to see you.'

'Yes, you are my soul mate. I will come by 03.30pm. Will it work?' She agreed finally.

'Hmmm...... I will finish my work by that time and wait for you for lunch. See ya.'

Her voice was broken and she seems to be too shaken, 16 months of disconnect

was too painful for both of us. She must have been through a tough time and have taken a lot of courage to connect with me again.

It was her last words 16 months back on phone when she was crying and cursing me,

Telling me that she never wanted to see me again, but I knew, we are made for each other. I have a family so I have distractions, she is alone.

The amount of her sufferings cannot be imagined.

As I sat in the cab and closed eyes, my mind went back many years in timeline.

At precisely 3.00 p.m. Jyshri walked into my clinic, she straightway entered my chamber, as now my staff also remembers her as a very important person in my life.

She is the same, broad forehead, rimless glasses covering mesmerizing eyes, a little bit thin, carrying same killer smile and the same black purse and same watch with fingers crossed in front of her torso. She was the same and she thought that I may not find her appealing, she was horribly wrong.

I have been dying to see her and here she was in one piece. I stood up from my chair and before I could move, she came running to embrace me, after ensuring that the wooden door of my chamber was closed.

Moments later I feel her tears flowing on my shirt. I lift her chin, her eyes are closed but giving way to tears, removing her glasses

I kiss her eyes; she holds me tighter as if never want to leave.

I kiss her forehead; she shudders as this has always been one point which arouses her.

Demanding more she opens her mouth, her right leg lifts and wraps me.

After some time, she opens her eyes and speaks, "You are a scoundrel, let me die in your arms rather than alone."

My lips shut her up. It seemed that time of past 2 years was spinning centrifugally, and all emotions wanted to drown in our hearts.

After a long and intimate kiss, we look into each other's eyes and hug again,

I let her go and grab my chair.

She too sat on the chair facing me and looked at me for a good one minute and then spoke that I have become leaner, there is not much difference except that I have lost fat and that my hair has grown grey.

I was just listening, but my mind was fast analyzing this woman.

"Ok tell me how are you, and how were you before coming here?

You seem to be OK physically, but I can sense the storm which has passed."

"It has not passed but has devastated my life." Came the reply.

"Where is Vikrama Nand?" I asked about her partner, "Why you guys never married?"

"It's a long story, he is still there but you very well know that I will never marry him as he has betrayed me by keeping his children with him and not letting his wife take custody. You were right in saying that if I have to marry him, I will marry with his baggage in the form of his parents, relatives and children.

I thought that he loved me and will leave everyone for me, but I think I am a time pass to him, a commodity for which he can boast of when he is in his friend circle.

Why did I not marry you? I will curse myself for whole of my life." She took sips of Limca from her purse, and offered me but I declined, as usual.

"As if life was simple to me when I got MDP (maniac depressive psychosis). You are one of the biggest reasons because you never cared about me. I was broke, Vikram gives me 15000/- rupees for a month from our consultancy earnings. I stopped working when psychosis overpowered me. When you are alone and vulnerable everyone wants to take advantage in the name of help. One of my close uncles (maternal) offered me money to sleep with him, saying that he will make me his *Rani*, he molested me.

He came to pay a regular visit to mom and asked about me and that he has never seen me in ages, mom said that I was not well and was in the room upstairs, he climbed 2 flights of stairs on the pretext of seeing me. I was all alone, he came inside the room and sat on my bed besides me suddenly his had was on my thighs I could not retaliate, I became numb, he left after showing me a bundle of currency notes giving me an offer to shift into one of his houses where I will get all the comforts for being his sex slave, later my mom told me to shut my mouth as no one would believe me and also then you were not there to support.

My uncle asked me to become his mistress, he said he will give me a separate flat to live, I was wasting my time in this makeshift arrangement with my mom. He is cunning and has molded my mom to believe in him and has got her signatures on property papers and snatched our property also.

I could not handle and lost my mental balance for a long time. I was alone, I became aloof. I stopped going down to my mother for anything and used to sit in my room looking at ants crawling on walls.

But my desire to meet you kept me alive. You would laugh on me if I told you that during my high mental status whenever I was out on streets, I used to hug strangers like *rickshawwala or shop keeper or thelawala out* of frustration and fear of dying."

After a pause which left me gazing at her speechless, not knowing why I was being crucified, never cared to interrupt her, she spoke again but now in a low tone.

"I had lost interest in sex and love, but when you kissed me just now, I became wet as earlier." She looked at me with mix feelings of blushing and smiling.

"I do not want you to leave your family but please be with me, I need you emotionally and maybe physically. I have become a dead person in both."

"Why do you say so? You had everyone except me, and that too you stopped answering my calls and messages. I tried to reach out to you, but you were not there.

You have my support always; you know that but ...."

She kept her finger on my lips and shook her head, "No complaints mister.

And I am not cursing you. You are the only one who has given me the meaning of love, rest everyone has treated me like a *rakhel*, and I am here after realizing that

I was wrong. Now please love me, I need you."

I already had fixed all my appointments for late evening.

We walked into my nursing homes' room where I take a power nap during day and started finding the missing pieces of time of togetherness of the past two years, filling up the blanks in our lives with emotions and physical love.

While making out in the room I found that the scar on her soul was deep, she was hurt and it reflected in the lovemaking, she was not enjoying, was not wet down there as she used to be and was lost somewhere.

I got off her and cuddled her to make the situation livelier, but she seemed to be lost somewhere.

"What happened *jaan*?" I stroked her hair; my other hand found her nipple which was flat and despite fiddling, it never cared for muscular action leading to an erection. I was however ready with my manhood.

"You are not here with me."

"I am here only; see you are complaining again. I am with you on your bed completely nude, you are kissing me, have intimately entered me and you think you are doing it in your imaginations."

"Ha,ha,ha I used to imagine making out with you daily, but you seem to be lost. Can I help you somewhere?"

"Remember I told you that you may not find me appealing.

All men in my life except you have used me as you guys use a condom, you are the only person who despite me showing interest in a relationship never took advantage.

It started with Himanshu, then that Lawyer who was married but as I did not have money for divorce proceedings, took advantage, making me a fool for marriage and raped me many times at my rented flat. And then as if Vikram was waiting for the right opportunity, remember I came to you for warts removal, he paid the bill and for next 3 months he too physically used me, his wife came to know about us and left him, he said he will marry me, but I cannot take responsibility of a preformed family and children who are not mine. Sorry for not giving you the same pleasure,

I do not think that I will be the same woman again." Moist eyes glued to the ceiling and face without expression gave the reply.

"What did you eat today?" I enquired just to change topic.

"Nothing, I am fed up of eating the same for breakfast, lunch and dinner.

Mom never prepares different meals as she has her girlfriend circle to gossip and her son for whom she can cook in mid of the night. I am a nobody living on her head, you know I pay the electricity bill for my room and for my DTH.

She even cries for the water I am using. I want to move out from there." She turned to look at me with a questionable look, "I know you can solve my problems, but you show such indifference towards me."

"Your brother did not get married or what?"

"You know *na* that he is disabled, finding a disabled match is not easy.

I love my brother, but I need my space and dignity."

Which you have been repeatedly losing in the hands of males who rape you or keep an hungry eye on you.

"And how is your friend, that cardiologist who treated your father?"

I wanted more skeletons to come out of the cupboard.

"He is nice, do you know that after you refused to give me money for a floor, I had a conversation with him, and he gave me keys of his vacant flat in front of his wife and both of them insisted that I should shift there.

But as it is far away in a deserted corner of sector 30 Rohini, I never went there.

He is a good fellow who even was ready to do the renovation according to my taste and later offered me a cash sum of five lakhs for living expenses."

"Was the transaction done in front of his wife?"

"No, she was in the hospital delivering a difficult case of maternity. He must have informed her later on as I went to his place sometimes later for tea when she was there too."

"Why do you ask?" Her eyes were filled with innocence.

"*Meri jaan tu bahut bholi hai aur abhi tak nahi samajh paayi ki tujhe sab istemaal karna chahte hain.* He seems to be smart; you must have shared your story with him too. I do not understand as why you want to cling to Vikram, he is not marrying you, he is not adding any value to you, people near your residence or who know you take your position to be his keep or mistress in their mind even your sisters think that way, why you do not get married to someone else?"

"I want you in my life, when you cannot be mine as I do not want to break your family,

I have to settle with him. I cannot adjust anywhere else you know that." I took her hand and put it on my penis asking to stroke as it was losing hardness due to our never ending discussion.

She took it but was very rough in handling my request as if she was punishing me for everything. I moaned in pain and took her nipple between teeth to reciprocate.

"Why are you so rough?" I was now panting.

"I want you to be fully prepared before you enter me and give me what I want."

She was adamant, climbed upon me, opened her legs and started to jump and thrust, she kept on jumping as if she was taking revenge of her life. I left her bosom and held her by buttocks as I was about to come. Suddenly she cried a loud shriek and a heavy load of her love juices which I call nectar started flowing. I also ejaculated after a few moments.

She lay her face on my chest and panting heavily uttered, "You are too good, I missed you so much."

"You did not have sex in between?" I asked.

"I had on 2 occasions with him, but it was not fruitful, we went to Agra for the same but I never enjoyed." She was still gasping and speaking in a hoarse voice. "*Tumhari to baat hi alag hai.*" She started kissing my nipples which started giving another hard-on.

I soaked my fingers in her nectar and inserted into her butt hole, which gave her an electric shock. We did it again when I saw her watch to find that it was time to do the clinical practice.

"Does he know that you are here?"

"*Pagal ho kya*, I have told him that an aunt has come from England, and I am meeting her."

"One day he will come to know about us." I said jokingly.

"That will be the last day of my life." Came a serious reply.

"Ok relax, I will finish off my clinic in one hour and then we

will go for dinner somewhere. I will lock the room from

outside, give me a tinkle if you need something."

I left her in the room to finish my clinic. After one and half hours when I opened the room, I saw her lying on the bed naked, looking at her mobile phone.

"Hi babe, you are not ready for dinner, are you not hungry?"

She smiled and made a gesture to come near to her and said in a hoarse voice, "I am ready for everything. Come make love to me." We did again and then I lifted her in my arms and took to the wash area where in the large mirror we appreciated our nakedness. While taking bath together, which we often do after sex, she held me tight and said, "Never leave me."

"Do you remember the first time we took a bath together?"

She asked still mingled with my torso.

"Yes, how can I forget? You came with full bushes down there and wanted me to examine for any recurrence of warts, for which I shaved your pubic hair. I had asked you to do it before visiting but you said that due to cervical pain you could not bend down so I shaved and lifted you in my arms before taking you to the wash area. You never resisted and let me wash, my clothes got drenched, and you started removing them."

She planted her lips to seal my voice. Later in the evening, we settled for Taj Vivanta's Indian restaurant, chose a seat aloof from most of the ambience and ordered. She took few selfies of our kisses before the starter drinks were served, vodka with lemon for her and I ordered single malt whiskey.

"How are you sure these pics will be safe from the public eye?"

"You know Vikram checks my phone daily, but he does not have access to my hidden folders." She said proudly. While drinking she looked down at the table for a long time.

"What is going in your mind, babe?"

"Multiple things, like you have become more muscular, and have lasted longer today.

You have satisfied my need for love. I was labelled as a slut, a gold digger, a whore *a rakhel* but you have given me the same respect as a lover would give.

Over past 10 years I have had more sexual intimacy opportunities with you than anyone else." She took a sip of the drink and continued.

"I do not get that much wet now as you would have experienced, it seems that the urge for physical relation and satisfaction is dying." "Yes, you are very less wet down there, but I love the juices, it is my favorite." I replied.

"Things will get to original self in a few days, I will take you out of this difficult phase." After a brief pause between us, she continued, "Why you still use local undergarments? I will buy you undergarments of UCB or US Polo association or Jockey make, I have amazon account active and will order. I have heard from

Vikram that they are more comfortable, and I think that will hide the stretch lines you have."

Probably second round of vodka was showing its effect, I kept listening. After another round of drinks, we started watching our love making on my phone which was recorded through CC TV cameras installed at my place.

When the food arrived, she stopped me from using the cloth napkin lying on table and demanded for tissues.

Most of our tastes match except that she does not like food items which have Vitamin C and also south Indian delicacies. She has an eye to catch the freshness of the food kept in plate, and she is never wrong.

"One of my known neighbors works for a five-star hotel in Bikaji Kama Place and says that these napkins are seldom washed properly and we unknowingly use them on lips & face."

I had to admit to the doubt about cleanliness.

Chapter 5

The beginning

10.09.2007

She is the 5th patient on my list of morning hours of practice. I have personally written as appointment was taken on my personal number. Jayshri, 26 years, female, resident of Rohini Delhi the appointment form read her details.

A thin, small built about 5 feet, fair colored, wearing plastic rim spectacles, a small black *bindi* on forehead, a feeble smile on lips, dark brown hair clad female enters my chamber, carrying a black lady's purse dangling on her right forearm.

It seemed to me that I had seen this young lady somewhere, maybe in a hospital or some marketplace but as my memory about people and their names is not so bright, so I stopped contesting the thought. This is the same lady who occupies my phone book named Anamika.

After asking her to sit comfortably on the patient seat, I asked her about reports of the investigations as instructed on phone before visiting me for her warts problem.

"Your report indicates that you have contracted some contagious sexually transmitted disease as in Herpes genitalis, Genital warts & trichomoniasis.

The good news is that HIV status is non-reactive meaning you do not have HIV infection." There is a silence……..she is sitting in front. From flat expressions on her face when I was narrating the reports to change of expressions and redness of eyes, it seemed to age.

Then Niagara Falls started, albeit silently.

"Relax!" I produced tissue box in front of her.

One, two & three…….

She took 3 tissues and put them on eyes before breaking down to sobs. She seems to be too much disturbed which any patient is bound to be. This a usual scene with some patients of both gender in whose consciousness guilt and a dreadful non treatable, life-threatening disease fear starts cropping up more, the positive reports give more fire power to the already guilt and fear feeling mindset.

"If you have something to tell me please go ahead, as these reports indicate that the infections can be present for a short time, and some can be there since a long time. As you said that you are separated from your husband for more than 2 years, the whole picture is a bit mix up."

I added further seeing no response but silent sobs, "It is Ok to get disturbed by the news of a contagious infection, but good part is that all are treatable."……………………

"And if you think that unloading your thoughts before me can lighten you, I am a sponge." Moist eyes looked at me, a thin smile erupted on her lips. Her face was full of emotions, I could make out helplessness, hatred, and dejection but a ray of the fighting spirit was battling, trying to overpower all emotions with the help of her killer smile.

"You are a good human being Sir. No doubt I had a crush on you when I consulted you in 2005 for my pimples before my marriage."

Bang!!! Now it was my turn of emotions with strange feelings to join the circus.

"What did you just say? Crush on me, when how? I barely know you."

"Who says if you do not know me then I do not have the liberty of liking you or loving you?" Now suddenly, her face was mixed with blush and pride.

"Many film stars do not know us, but people fall in love with them *hai na*." I nodded at her crisp point but to make her comfortable from her newly diagnosed disease burden I took a plunge into our conversation about me.

"When I consulted you for my pimples, you were slightly plump and the way you explained after signing the prescription, it was an out of the world experience to me. You took all the time to explain, and I was constantly looking at your face, not listening but falling in love with you."

She took a breath and continued, "Generosity from a smart looking, well learned male would make any girl weak on knees. I have been looking for such a partner for whole of my life."

Now, this was another shock to me, if my explanation could catch eye of a good looking female then I will be in eyes of many such beauties which I never knew.

"But you never expressed your feelings to me. I was a bachelor at that time. You could have changed the course of your life" I smiled.

"I did not dare to ask you anything thinking that your position as a doctor is far ahead of me, and I never knew you were single." She giggled.

Now she seemed to be at ease.

"After that consultation, when I reached home,

I kept laughing at myself as I did not understand the medicines."

"Later in the evening after I had purchased the same from nearby chemist,

I rang up your clinic number to talk to you and to my good fortune you picked up and were very courteous in explaining the application method again.

That was the golden act and I kept imagining you speaking with closed eyes till I fell asleep." She was now looking down towards her feet or maybe the floor.

"I am sure you would have imagined me more. So at least I left a mark in your mind, and you have consulted me again because of the memory as a doctor or may be as your crush" I teased her.

"You have made a permanent impression on my mind and a permanent place in my heart, and I trust you, so I have come to you." She was a bit irritated.

"I later found Himanshu, my husband, and was in a relationship with him sans physical intimacy before marrying him. I remember and I will never forget that before our marriage, it was my birthday and no one had wished me, not even Himanshu. I was feeling heart broken when you called up to wish me. Your call and voice were a *shockingly* happy moment I was dying for, although after getting into a relationship,

I had forgotten about you. That made my day and I was so happy after your short birthday wish that I forgave Himanshu." She was beaming into that day's memories.

"I wish all my patients on birthdays as a good gesture, but my call saved him, and I can see in my records that your phone number listed is not working and you have acquired a new Airtel number." I chuckled.

"But what was the reason for bitterness in your fairy tale relationship?" An obvious query from my side.

And then I wanted to narrow down to the origin of so many STDs, not needed for consultation but for proper treatment and bit of curiosity. There was a silence, her face showed sea of emotions from happy moments turning into rough tides.

Finally, she uttered. "Will I be cured?" Her questionable gaze was telling that there is a lot behind those beautiful eyes.

Pulling 3 tissues from the box seems to be her signature move to take tissues as she repeated the maneuver many times and I kept the count of 3 on every pull. After a while she stopped crying.

Out of my medical and humanitarian curiosity, I asked "Ok, if you want to tell me more about you or the infections, I am all ears. This will make you light, probably .....eh and will guide me further to write the treatments. Otherwise,

I can sign the prescription without that also."

She took out a bottle of limca hidden in her purse and after some sips looked at me.

"I don't know why I am telling you this story of my life, but it seems most appropriate at the present moment of my life. And moreover, I have both feelings and trust as far as you are concerned"

Meanwhile I checked my watch, it was 1 pm and I was supposed to go for lunch, I thought that it will take another few minutes before I finish with the story and that's it.

Little did I know that it was the beginning.

"I met Himanshu through a common friend, I was working as a manager in an adhesive industry, drawing a good salary. In a few meetings I fell for him."

This is a standard plot out of a common Bollywood film, I thought looking at my watch.

She was staring at the bottle of limca and continued.

"We were doing great and decided to marry against our parents' wishes. As I am the eldest among 4 of us, my mother was dead against my decision.

She has never supported me since the time I remember. I tried my level best to win over her but all in vain, I fought for him, I cared for him even when he was not earning.

Then I came to know about another girlfriend, who he introduced to me and told that he has slept with her. Being physical was never my priority before marriage, so probably he was looking around. We stopped speaking to each other but after 3 months one fine day he said sorry, asked me to meet him at a common joint, brought the girl and asked me to marry him in front of her. I was shocked and surprised, he took my hand in front of her and asked me to marry him, and that swept me off the ground.

We married within a week of that incident in front of the marriage registrar, and I footed the bill of our rented accommodation and furniture."

"Oh...... so you had a difficult start, but what is the connection of all these infections with this? You say that you are separated from your husband for last 2 years." I again peeped at my watch as my gastric juices reminded me of the empty spaces where the juices were grunting.

"He was not the one who has given me these warts" a cold reply as if coming from a hollow vessel distracted my vision and thoughts.

"He went to Bangkok with friends and did not call me once from there, he enjoyed with sex workers and after a week came back to me, that night he asked me to perform a nude dance for him while he was drinking.

He even forced me to drink whiskey. After some time when he was ready, he ordered me to do oral on him. When I took him in my hands, I felt something was not right and saw some wounds there. We did nothing after that, and I asked him to see you next morning."

Another pause and sip of Limca before she began.

"After 2 days of persuasion, he came to see you and you had advised him treatment for genital herpes infection and asked for some blood tests.

He lied to me that you have given him a clean chit. I got the correct information when I saw your prescription in his wallet. He left me again for a month saying that he was on a business trip. Later I came to know that he was staying at Bhera enclave at his parents' place."

Flood of emotions broke all the rules and flowed freely on her cheeks. My tissue box was being lightened of its content 3 pulls every time.

"After coming from his parent's place, he brought some of his friend's home and had a party whole night with free-flowing alcohol. I was not interested so went to other room in our 2-room flat after some time and slept, thinking that he has met his friends after a long time so let them enjoy with their same age-old talks.

At 3 am in the morning I heard as someone was making out in my house. I unlocked my room to see my husband in briefs and one of his friends getting intimate with a call girl whom they had arranged under the influence of alcohol, when I was not in their vision. Seeing me, Himanshu made an excuse that he did not do anything, but his friends were only enjoying. In a fit of rage, I shouted on everyone there and asked them to leave immediately, saw the naked girl laughing at me as if they all were regular into all this. That morning I left for my mom's place, where I knew that I will not be accommodated for long time. But my daddy took the decision to make me stay at their place till I wanted. Mom was never in my favor for anything since childhood and myself marrying in such a manner made her a stranger for me."

She had caught me looking at my watch and said, "Please give me medicines and I will come later to get the warts removed, you must be busy."

"I would like to examine the warts or whatever it is before I can prescribe anything.

Are you comfortable? My staff will be there."

"Do I have a choice of saying no? And I have requested you to treat my problem, and here I am telling you all my story of life gone wrong." She spoke with a clear sense of dejection.

After her nod for examination, I asked the nurse to take her to the procedure room where I have an examination table.

Meera, the nurse, changed the disposable sheet on the bed, gave Jayshri a disposable gown before calling me to examine her.

She was lying down on her back with tightly shut but moist eyes, fists clenched, and jaw muscles tightened.

"Relax, I am not going to kill you or harm you.

I will see the warts in question for which your gynecologist has referred.

I will do the procedure later if it is required and when you are ready for the same." I laughed a bit in order to relax her.

Meera held her hand as a reassuring gesture and spoke to calm her.

Slowly she was in a better position.

"You have visited the Gynecologist also; I am a skin doctor,

and we use smaller instruments whenever required."

I gestured Meera to give her position so that I could examine her in proper light.

When the gown was lifted, her hairy legs welcomed my gaze.

As per my telephonic instruction the other day, she had shaved only on the pubic area.

Nurse took her to proper position for examination and adjusted the OT light,

I could see florid cauliflower-like small lesions masking the labia majora.

"Now I will be examining manually, take a deep breath and open legs as wide as possible."

I said wearing 2nd layer of gloves.

After examining the outer lips, I separated the same and looked at the pinkish inner lips or labia minora, there dark colored verrucae were filling the space extending to the introitus.

She winced and moved her hips as the steel speculum entered her vaginal opening. She was wet down there so the speculum could easily be guided inside.

Adjusting the headlight with my forearm, I found some more verrucae inside the vaginal canal.

"It is over, now you can relax. I will remove them with carbon dioxide laser under local anesthesia."

"How much will it cost?" A low tone voice asked from the examination table.

"The whole procedure will cost you five thousand five hundred rupees and will take about thirty minutes."

I waited for her response. Generally, patients start bargaining as if they have come out to buy vegetables. No one will ask for a discount on alcohol, *paan* or other things which harm pocket and health being a double-edged sword, but the same people will become poor in paying to doctor or for medicines where asking discount becomes their birthright.

Anyways, I cannot change state of mind in general as I am not a social worker or a politician.

"How long will it take to heal doctor?" She broke my thoughts.

"Usually, after laser you will be able to do everything as usual, except intercourse for 7 days, which probably is a wrong advice to you. By the way you must have brought sanitary napkin for the post procedure dressing which I have asked you on the phone, please hand it over to the staff." I started removing gloves to change again to set the laser machine.

Looking at my watch, I knew that I was getting late for my lunch and my wife would get worried, but I wanted to finish the laser today itself. She caught me staring at the watch and rose from the table to change to her clothes and said, "Sir you must be getting late, I will come later for the removal."

"No, it's OK, we can do the laser procedure today itself, I can do it after lunch. Would you like to get the procedure done?" a child caught in an innocent act of looking again at watch can utter this much.

"I am not carrying enough money for the laser, so I will come some other day." "Is there no other alternative to laser? I am afraid of the word laser operation."

Came a voice from inside the changing room.

"Laser is the quickest and safest, some of the other alternatives includes applying acid, or some medicines which will burn and will make you limp for two to three weeks and in case you get your periods during such times, imagine the difficulty.

Before lasers were developed, we doctors used to treat with such methods only" I cleared her doubts.

"You are free to change your mind, but I can assure you that with lasers, you are in one of the safest hands in our country."

"Ok doctor, thank you very much but I will surely come again for the treatment later". She said before collecting the prescription, after reading her name printed as Jayshri, she requested me to correct it to JYSHRI.

Some times later she informed me that her astrological name is Jyotsna but believing in numerology she has changed it to Jyshri.

Many patients do not give their correct name and we have no other option but to write the given name.

I obliged her personal choice and issued a new prescription. I too collected the cash and asked my multipurpose staff to take me home for lunch.

We had driven only few hundred meters when I saw a familiar figure walking slowly towards the entry of nearby Haldiram store, it was the same feminine figure who has declined to get warts treated.

Few days passed as usual, I got busy with my routine schedule and family. One day, I heard my receptionist speaking to someone in a loud sarcastic tone "*agar ye aapke husband nahi hain to kaun hai?*"

Looking on the screen of my CCTV, I saw Jyshri sitting on one chair of the waiting area with other patients and a thin-built male standing near the reception table looking embarrassed.

"Meera do not be loud" I called my secretary cum nurse on intercom and asked to send the patient to my chamber.

When her turn came, she entered my chamber, leaving her male accomplice outside. After a few moments of explaining the procedure, I asked my secretary to accompany Jyshri to the procedure room and give a changing gown.

While I donned the surgical gown, cap, mask and surgical gloves, the nursing staff cleaned the area of her genitals and gave me the laser probe.

"Is he known to you?" I was curious about the accompanying person whom my secretary has asked an annoying question.

"Yes, he is my partner."

"Oh, live-in partner, is it?"

"No, no we work together." Came reply from lips with a tinge of fear of the procedure.

Since her eyes were blinded with a plastic goggle and gauge, I could not make out as what was going on there.

"So, what kind of work you do now."

I keep asking questions to all patients who are on the procedure

table to reduce their anxiety and make them comfortable in the laser maneuver.

"I.. we do consult services." Came a dry reply.

She was not yet relaxed.

"Oh great, what consultation you guys provide? I used to think that only doctors, lawyers, or chartered accountants give consultancy services." I prepared fresh local anesthesia in tuberculin syringes which have the easily available thinnest needles.

“Madam I am going to inject local anesthesia on the skin affected and it will feel like deep pinch. You may take a deep breath and you are free to ask me to stop if the procedure is painful.”

The wart removal took less time than I thought. The nurse cleaned and dressed the wound and asked the patient to wait in the post procedure area for observation. I went back to my chamber and finished a consultation with two other patients.

My consultation room is at a distance from the procedure room, and it becomes easier for me to do procedures even if a child or anyone else

is shouting out of fear of injections etc. as the voice does not create panic in those waiting for consultation or procedures.

Her accompanying person was sitting in the waiting area reading magazines, never looked up probably embarrassed because of receptionist's question.

After half an hour nurse brought the patient to my chamber, she was feeling slight pain.

I prescribed a set of medicines as post procedure and asked to come back after 05 days for checkup. Jyshri left with a promise in her eyes to report on the follow-up date after paying at the reception counter.

In my career I have removed many warts and have treated patients for sexually transmitted diseases, but this patient was different.

Her story has made an impression on my mind, and I wanted to know more, as many pieces were not fitting together. Maybe she was cooking up a story which seemed unlikely, given the number of emotions that changed gears while she narrated her ordeal.

Chapter 6

Gaj Gamini

It has been more than one year since I removed her warts. She is here at a prescribed time for another checkup of warts. Now after more than one year of knowing, we are regularly on phone calls, at least for a few hours we keep discussing life and its repercussions on our lives. We do not discuss politics or gadgets, but our talks are generally about her life. Incidentally all 4 staff members of the clinic had decided to go for a movie in adjoining Fun Cinemas, I knew my schedule did not have any patient, and so

I gave early leave to my staff who were very happy for the same and I could utilize the time to study some journals and write literature.

“No one is there at the clinic? Where are your staff members?” She wanted to know but was showing comfort in her voice.

“Oh, they wanted to go for a new tabloid in nearby theatre, and since no patient was scheduled, I thought of revising the book I am writing.

It is a pleasant surprise that you are here.”

“Oh, I have stopped you from reviewing the book you told me about some time back, my bad. But tell me about the book, you have kept it a secret, now we are friends, you can share the content with me.” She demanded.

"I am at midway on the same, and let it be a surprise for everyone. I hope that your warts are not troubling you anymore." She nodded and asked me to examine once more for any recurrences. So, after an exchange of pleasantries, we moved to the procedure room.

"Doc, *aap mujhe puri body par examine kar lo, kahin bhi warts ho to treat kar do.*"

She was looking into my eyes.

"Ok, so you will have to remove all your clothes and change into this disposable gown." I replied handing over the gown, which she dropped on the bed and spoke "*agar gown me hi examine karna hai to in kapdo me hi kar lo.*"

"As you wish."

"But no, *koi bhi wart reh gaya to phir se ho jayenge. Aap pura examine karlo please.*"

The way she was putting up the request, it seemed a proposal to touch her body.

"Ok, let's start." I started donning gloves.

"Gloves *se nahi pata chalega*. I won't mind if you do it without gloves.

I myself try to find with fingertips and nail."

I suddenly stopped and removed the partially worn glove, and looked at her.

"Sure, as you say. But warts are highly contagious and may make my hands infected."

She removed her top, then the white trouser she was wearing, this time her legs were clean, but her lower back showed a big bunch of fine hair just above the waist.

It looked like a faun tail, but her gait was normal as I have observed. Her site in skin colored bikini started giving me a hardon which she was staring.

"I may become uncomfortable during the examination, do not worry." Catching her gaze, I uttered.

"I do not fear you." She giggled and turned around to remove her panty, her butt cheeks started shining in front of me. Her hands tried to find the bra clip with hesitation which led my hands to assist her. My touch made her shiver, and she clasped my hands and took them forward on her boobs.

We made love for next one hour. This was the first time I had with her. She was amazing, great kisser, lots of love juices flowing out and she held me inside her for a long warm shower. We did in various positions, and she seemed to enjoy each with masterly perfection, although she was hesitant in asking for more.

While moaning with pleasure, she kept on saying that she loves me. She thanked me profusely and said that her wish for having intimacy with me is now fulfilled.

After taking a shower together in the wash area of my procedure room, I said, "Now should I examine you for warts or not."

"I thought you have done that in past long hours of love, haven't you?" She smiled. "Promise me that you will never use a glove or a condom with me."

I took her inside the whole body PUVA chamber and pretended to examine her, she took a sensual pose and said "Gaj Gamini, I am gaj gamini and you are my artist."

"Your artist will never use gloves or condom with you, promise."

"I have a fantasy." I spoke.

She looked into my eyes with a demand to shell out quickly. "I will fill your belly button with red wine and drink from there, under candle lights whenever we make love at home or on holiday."

"Your Gaj Gamini is dying for that moment."

"Ok does my Gaj Gamini has some fantasies."

"Yes, many of them."

"I want to make love on the kitchen table. While you drive car,

I want to sit on the rear seat, hug and kiss you from behind.

I see our daughter talking to you and you running with her.

I imagine you doing some grinding with mixer grinder in kitchen when I hug you from behind and the whole paste is splashed upon us and the walls, when we are making out on terrace, I want to smear your love juice on whole of my body............"

"Oh, so many, for these we may have to wait." I spoke.

"I have been waiting for you for so many births and ages."

Came a reply, she was looking at the blank wall.

Before I could ask or say anything she said that she had visited a past life regression therapist somewhere who had shown her to be my lover in past 4 lives, but we were not married. In one life we both took a plunge from a high mountain, in another one she was a dancer in the court of a king, and I was the *vaid* of the king, in 5th birth from now we were married, and I was a practicing ayurvedic physician, in another era she was my nurse.

So, this is the reason of her belief that we are soul mates.

I do not believe on any of such past life regression etc. activities and think that all these are money making tactics of the so-called therapists, but she seemed to believe in them.

The same or many other therapists and future tellers had told her that she will never marry and will remain unsatisfied with her life.

Gaj gamini seems to be a strange beauty.

Chapter 7

WhatsApp call at 3.14 am

I am at Bhubhneshwar for a meeting of IADVL (Indian Association of Dermatologists, Venereologists & Leprologists) an official association of Skin specialists of India.

As soon as the aircraft landed at the Biju Patnaik International Airport, my cell phone gave a buzz indicating that I have missed some calls. As usual, alighting from the aircraft from my favorite seat 1C smoothly and boarding the bus for terminal area, cellphone started ringing.

"Have you reached safely?" She was on the other side. It is 6.40pm and the weather is pleasant.

Her voice seemed cool.

In past few years we have become part of each other's lives.

"No, I am coming back to home, I forgot my tickets." I laughed.

"I have just landed here at Bhubhneshwar and am going to hotel. I wish you were here with me."

"You know I have a fear of heights, I cannot fly, still you keep teasing me. I am missing you so much."

"Ok baba, we will not fly but will drive in car as we did earlier for

Jaipur and other places, let me reach the hotel and then we will talk." I tried to calm her while boarding the taxi after locating the driver who was holding a placard with my name.

"Any one is with you?"

"Yes, the driver is with me, and you are with me always."

In 30 minutes of drive, I was at the reception of Mayfair Gardens resort.

Having informed at my home that I landed safely, I rushed to my room to freshen up.

Before I could take clothes out, my phone rang.

"Hi, *aap ne to call nahi kiya*. I have been waiting so I thought I must call you.

Have you reached the hotel? As there is no traffic noise, I am making a guess."

"Your guess is correct; I am in my room and am going to take a shower before I go for dinner."

"Show me the room *na*. It will give me a feel that I am with you. You always show me the room wherever you go."

"Ok let's make a video call on Whatsapp." I suggested.

In next few minutes I took her to a tour of the resort, before returning to the room.

"Now I will get into shower. I will plant the phone at a secure place in the bathroom and will talk to you."

"No, I cannot see you taking a shower, I will miss our times together.

But I want to see you." She was desperate.

"Look I have brought the Jockey innerwear which you have purchased for me from Amazon, and I am going to wear the same tonight."

I showed her the Jockey briefs one by one.

Phantom was the nomenclature awarded to me as a reward.

After Shower show and finishing dinner of broccoli salad with smoked salmon and rice,

I thought of retiring for the night with morning schedule of hitting the gym and swimming pool of the resort in my mind.

It was 10 pm when I received her call on WhatsApp.

"After I saw you taking shower, I too went to my small so-called bathroom and took bath, thinking about you and then as usual went downstairs to find mom sleeping and the food of my share lying on kitchen slab,

I ate the available food and rushed to my room to see and talk to you." She was fast to give me all details.

"You were looking great in the phantom attire, next time we will purchase florescent ones."

"You want to make me a joker or something in the florescent undergarments?" I complained.

"No no no.... actually, while after I purchased for you, I stumbled upon fluorescent options on Amazon. By the way do you share your under garments with anyone?"

"No never, why do you say so?"

"*Haan mai bhi yahi soch rahi thi* but you know Vikram does not have any problem in sharing under garments, his nephew visited and stayed overnight and next morning he wore Vikram's under garments after shower.

No one in his house has any problem in that. They even eat without brushing teeth in morning. Strange that his father is a priest.

They are from Bihar and have many orthodox beliefs." She informed.

"Being from any state will not have these strange and disgusting attitudes,

I can only say this. And you want to spend life with him, great of you. By the way I do not speak any word before I brush teeth and that is my choice, so let it be comfortable for him the way he is." I teased.

"He has his family, his sister's family and parents to support, and you are a free soul who could not stay with your ex-in-laws, who does not want to cook but wants your mother to cook for you, how will you justify this?"

I was annoyed because more than 10 years of listening the same complaints, yet I do not want to leave him was too much.

"Tell me what is my option? I do not have money to settle alone, I am dependent on fifteen thousand rupees which he gives me, I am old now to bear children so no other person will marry me, I am old enough and no one would be interested in me.

I cannot work as a housewife for any new relationship, you are married so no chance with you who is the only person to have understood me, whole world knows me as keep of Vikram, my mom, my sisters, even my relatives, the shopkeepers in my area think that I am available for sex if I am not seen with someone,

I have wasted my life in waiting for some miracle, only hope was that he will leave his children and all other family members, but he refused flatly and spoke that I have to accept as it is, it was a blow to me." I kept silent.

"I never listened to your words of advice to marry someone else, I never wanted to be away from you. My mom thinks that I am a whore, she never takes me seriously, you know when I had developed warts and asked for her help, she did not give an ear to me,

I was broken but had to get it treated when I visited you."

"Vikram helped me in those 3 months and one day, under the influence of alcohol asked me for sex in lieu of the help extended to me. I had barely recovered from the trauma of divorce and rape by the lawyer when he struck an eye on me for sex.

His wife had left him for some other person. He was desperate to satisfy his hormones and he found me poor from all quarters, an easy prey who was looking for some stability in life. For six years he falsely pretended to be everything for me, showed that he was totally dependent upon me. Took me to hotels and exploited me physically in the name of love. My whole family knows this, and you are looking for an option? Is it not enough that we are together despite all this? I have been with you ever since I met you for the first time. There have been ups and downs in our relationship mainly because you have a family, but I do not complain."

Yes, truly there have been many ups and downs since 2008 in our relationship which has become a see-saw. Every time she has gone away from me, she has caught some or the other medical issue severe enough to kill. Be it warts in genitalia, depression, typhoid, flu, or bipolar disorder.

Her sobs continued for a long period. I kept myself silent as I wanted her emotions to come out lest she went into a nervous breakdown.

She started opening up layer by layer about Mussoorie trip, Vikram and his wife. She continued with heavy voice and too heavy emotions, "When I first met Vikram, he was married, had one kid and was working in a share trading firm. We became friends and I used to visit his home some time. My married life was on the verge of breaking down, I was separated from Himanshu and did not have guts to meet you and tell you that I am being a secondhand girl was interested in you."

"Vikram and his wife shared that they were not getting privacy time in the family and were planning to go for a vacation. He asked me to accompany, and I agreed seeing that his wife did not have any objection and I wanted a break from my turmoil.

We went to Mussoorie where my job was to take care of his toddler son so that they spent good times alone in their room. After returning from the short 3-day holiday, my visits to their home increased and soon his liking towards me became obvious to his wife which led to frequent quarrels between them. Finally, she left him and filed for divorce."

More sobs continued, I was glued to the bed and phone, listening to her story which was opening a new chapter of her life.

"My own family has abandoned me; I am staying at my mom's place because

I do not have anywhere to go. Do you know, my LPG cylinder connection is different from hers, our cable TV, electricity meter and moreover water tanks are also separate? No one will believe on my words. Except for rent and payment for food, everything is separate. For rent and food payment I buy groceries almost daily and still am considered an outsider. This attitude has been from the day I married Himanshu.

I know that none of my family members are with me when I need, but everyone wants my help. You must not know and would be surprised if I told you that mom had breast cancer, diagnosed and operated some 15 years ago. It was followed later on by multiple consultations and she went for chemotherapy, I took her to various doctors and hospitals.

It took one and half years for her to stabilize, I had to leave my studies and job for her treatment. But when I developed typhoid, she practically dumped me in a nursing home, where a junior doctor tried to touch me at various places."

I was confused as what to say or not to say, any word from my side in favor or against any of her story characters would have jeopardized her mood.

I decided to keep quite except emit monosyllables 'hu' 'ha'.

As if a movie is playing in front of my eyes and the director will ask for my verdict on any scene, I was attentive to each word, in the mid of night.

"When I was going through trauma of divorce, Vikram was helping me, as I did not get any help from my mom or other family members, so I started helping him morally and stated giving him tips. You can understand that when two persons are facing similar situation in life, it is natural to develop sympathy and feelings.

Since I was not having any one in my life and you were a distant dream,

I took this as my destiny and agreed to his physical relations demands. I had discussed with him the sexual assault by my lawyer, and he seemed ok with it rather he went to threaten the lawyer for his deeds."

There was a brief pause, but I kept listening.

"We used to book room in local hotels for his physical needs. I mistook that he would abandon his family and children for me and marry me. When the time of settlement of his divorce case came; he took the custody of his children and never discussed it with me. I was there for him for six years, became his mistress, never married again thinking that he understands me, but later only I realized that he was using me.

Now you tell me that for a divorced girl, after long years of divorce, when everyone in the family and relatives know that I am involved with a divorcee and go out of station for vacations with him, who will marry me? I thought that Vikram understands me but now I have realized that he wants me in his life on his terms and conditions. He very well knows that I cannot stay in a family, I cannot do any household work, and that I want to live a good life, and that I do not have any support. He has taken advantage of the same and has made my life totally dependent on him. He boasts about his influence upon me when he is with his friends drinking. Now I cannot go out of my room without his knowledge. I delete all the call logs after I talk to you because he checks my phone many times in a day. I am trapped like a whore, a mistress and you are exploring options for me. There is no option but to.........."

Suddenly phone went silent. It was 03.14 am.

Thinking that it could be network issue, I called her through WhatsApp, she disconnected. Then I called her through phone call, she disconnected.

After waiting for some time, I dozed off.

My mobile ring tone woke me up.

04.36 am. It is her phone call.

"You know Vikram was calling me. He must have seen that I am online on

WhatsApp and was calling me and that is the reason I disconnected.

I am afraid that he will demand an explanation which will be difficult for me to do.

Tell me what I should do?" She whispered; her tone was indicative that she is scared and if her vocal cords spoke in normal decibels, Vikram will listen.

"This is too much, tell him the truth about your feelings, the trauma of being with him, live your life, get out of this cage." I sounded rude.

"The day he comes to know about us will be last day of my life." She answered. "I was expecting a practical solution at this moment for his questions about my being online at 3 am."

"Simple, you can tell him that you slept late and forgot to switch off the internet connection and WhatsApp before sleeping, and that your mobile was on silent mode, so even if anyone calls, you will know only in the morning after waking up."

"Are you sure he will buy this excuse? I am afraid that he may ask airtel to furnish call details."

"If you are so much so afraid of him, then we should stop talking for good.

Live your life, he is controlling you with a remote button of emotional torture, come out of it or ask him to marry you on your terms, otherwise your life will be difficult."

"Ok I will say as you are suggesting, hope that he does not poke further." She surrendered.

"Tell me how I was looking in the new spectacles which we got made at Titan eye plus?" I wanted to change the topic or to sleep desperately.

"You are smart and have become smarter. Muuha" she kissed me through phone.

Now I knew that she will be at ease for her fears.

Rest of the morning was spent in long talks and at six thirty I went for gym and swimming, it was a heavy night and I wanted to be fresh before my main purpose of visiting Bhubhneshwar, meeting for a disease called psoriasis.

Chapter 8

Suicide by choice

Thud, thud, thud.......sound of chappals clad feet climbing stairs.

"*Haye meri beti, twanu ki hoya*"

A thin salwar kameej clad, wrinkled skin old female along with few neighbors are climbing stairs hurriedly in the hope of seeing that everything is alright.

Moments back Saurabh a tenant in the next-door 3rd floor apartment had called her name loudly.

Saurabh, living with 2 of his room partners friends on the 3rdfloor of rented accommodation to study was awake at usual time to witness the hot female neighbor from the window.

The buildings are constructed on 30-meter plots and are such that one can jump from one terrace to another without any major effort.

It is situated in a thickly populated residential colony of North Delhi called Rohini.

Saurabh and his friends felt lucky to have a view of the adjacent second floor where a short height, divorced beautiful female is living in a one room settlement.

The kitchen and small bathroom are separate with a passage of terrace in between the room and facilities. The bathroom has a metal door with open ventilation in the upper portion of the door.

From adjacent third floor one could easily see someone bathing up to the waist of the person taking a bath. Saurabh was lucky to have witnessed the *Didi* taking bath with full view of solid looking bosoms and shining skin. He used to see her daily and wished to do so forever. In past few months, the room rent increased, and his roommates changed but he never wanted to forego the sight of a female taking a bath for a few rupees.

He gave an excuse for rising inflation to his parents staying in the village and could convince them to bear extra expenses.

He had put a curtain on the window so that the unsuspecting female could not catch him watching her.

Poor guy was not aware of the female sixth sense, she knew of his deeds, and she used to enjoy imagining a young lad, looking at her body with pants down, getting hard on and shagging on the floor.

In past few months Saurabh had witnessed one bearded male accomplice visiting occasionally and staying for many hours inside the room with closed door.

He started feeling jealous of him but could not do any harm as the male friend was seen having chat with auntyji, mother of the young, divorced and hot female.

At 2 -3 occasion an old man with completely white hair had stayed for many hours inside the closed room with her.

Saurabh observed a common string, after each male spent a few hours, after seeing the person off downstairs, she used to come up, clean the room, wash bedsheets and take bath even if it was cold late evening.

This kept the young man confused. He could only imagine the pleasure exchanges inside the closed door and fume about the same, cursing his luck.

Money plays a major role in every trade, and this is the oldest trade known to humans. Many a times he wanted to jump over to the other side of the terrace to grab her and pin her down with door open inside her bedroom so that his friends could see them making out. Then he used to do it himself and relax.

Enough tension and tension relieving maneuvers.

Today as usual, he was ready for the show, hidden behind the curtains, usually, her voice talking to someone on phone with earphones dangling while she did daily tasks was the alarm that she will now enter the bath, mostly she used to speak loudly that she will call after getting ready, or that she will wait near the flower shop, or the police post in half an hour etc.

Today was not a usual day as he did not hear her voice.

Probably she is asleep.

But in the wee hours he had heard her brushing teeth, also there was a door slamming noise.

She seems to be a strange female, she is hot, beautiful, charming but her deeds of walking on the small area of terrace and her very long hours talks on phone, her shrieking voice to somebody on the other side, her sobs, her dance with earphones on was scary.

Often, she looked up to the window from where her young stalker

Saurabh used to make imaginative love with her, sometimes with no expression, sometimes with a smile and sometimes as if she is looking for him.

Suddenly there is a noise of something falling on the ground from her room and it is followed by a noise as if someone is gagging and gasping for air or strangulating came from her room.

Very recently series of suicides in Bollywood had shaken the world.

Saurabh started shouting

"*didi………………..didi……………..didi*"

He wasted no time when there was only a strange sound as if someone was gasping for air.

He started shouting again.

"*Aarey koi hai kya, auntyji, Bhabhi ji, bhaiya(his landlord) dekho Khili didi ko kya hua hai.*"

For the first time he has taken her name in public, the name with which she is famous in her neighborhood. With this he himself ran down shouting to alarm others.

As the area is very small, his shouting voice raised many ears and soon many foots were rushing towards the 2nd floor of his hot and sexy fantasies' floor.

As the door of his dream bedroom was thrown open by many hands, he saw Khili dangling from a fan hook with a thick cloth of *chunni* wrapped around her neck and tied in a knot, her hands trying to unwrap the knot, which seemed to get tight with every shake of her legs desperate to find a platform to stand. The stool she climbed before pushing it down the bed was lying there.

Her eyes were pooping out and her face was turning reddish blue.

He along with others , mostly females started crying, while his landlord held dangling torso and gave support when another neighbor climbed the bed to loosen the knot.

He ran out towards the kitchen outside her room to fetch water while other people helped Khili to lay down on the bed.

Auntyji (her mother) started beating her own chest and crying loudly, many neighbor aunties held her and consoled her that at least Khili was alive, and now has to be looked after.

"*Saadi to kismet hi phooti hai. Kalmuhi janamte hi mar jaati*." She started wailing a usual scene of cursing in a middle-class Punjabi family of Delhi.

When Saurabh returned to the room filled with neighbors with a glass of water from her kitchen, his landlady was sitting next to Khili holding her hands.

With teary voice, she spoke " *Didi aap theek ho na*."

His fantasy, now lying on the same dream bed, with full clothes on but with tears, red face and gasping breath, did not utter a single word but kept crying.

To add to her woes, auntyji kept on cursing her and her male accomplice for everything. Someone suggested to call police, some other person suggested calling a doctor.

I received a call from her number, but it was her neighbor speaking, request was to immediately visit her place as there had been an accident with Khili.

I am shocked to hear that and am asking more information about the accident when the connection broke and voice disappeared.

I called on the same number immediately.

Ring.....ring.....ring....ring, she opened her eyes to see that it is 7 am and the phone is ringing, it is her mother calling probably for breakfast.

It was a nightmare. One of the usual dream patterns which she sees at some intervals.

It seems to be an outcome of her thoughts and nihilistic behavioral changes.

Chapter 9

Birthday

"Curtains are drawn, now everything will be revealed on your birthday", I teased her.

"Why, are you making any plans?"

"Yes dear, something big I have thought of. I want you to wait till then."

She was looking at the windscreen of our car, lost in thoughts.

"Himanshu gave me so many cards, dolls, chocolates........" came a mumble.

"Be ready to have a memorable day" I tried her to focus on present day.

My efforts had to wrestle a tough fight but finally it won the battle.

"I am not comparing but you will remember your birthday with me till your memory lasts."

We finished the *nariyal paani* and started for the Rajouri Garden market parking space.

She has purchased a red overcoat and few under pants.

I made it clear that the overcoat is 1st in series of her birthday gifts.

It is still 5 days to her birthday.

Next, we went to a mall in Shivaji Nagar where she wanted to purchase a watch.

She settled on a watch by Gucchi as her 2nd birthday present.

By the evening, I made a nice invite about her birthday party and sent it on her WhatsApp.

It read as "You are cordially invited to join the birthday celebration of my jaan Jyshri on ------- at --------, followed by sumptuous lunch and music.

Dress code is Black formals including black undergarments, which will be changed to pink after the celebrations."

Incidentally her Brother-in-law was visiting the family during that evening, and her mobile was lying unattended on couch, seeing it light up after the

WhatsApp msg, he picked up the cell and asked her to open to see some photos.

She opened the phone and gave it to him, the first thing he saw was the invite!!!

Although she deleted the same after some time, but the message was seen. In her eyes damage was done.

I asked her to ignore any questionable looks from her sister's family and carry on.

After this incident, she asked me to invite Vikram also so that it would be easy for her to say that it is going to be a group celebration.

"Would that not give a message of group sex? Never mind I will invite him if you say so." I teased.

I made another sober invite and sent it to Vikram, called him not to reveal the venue.

On the day, I had made all arrangements of a room and lunch at The Lalit, Connaught Place, along with a musician and guitar player.

I reached near her house in the morning and called her to my car.

She came raw, without makeup etc. She had slept very late, courtesy our long chat and talks which started at 11.59 pm with me reciting the lines from Kabhi Kabhi written by poet Harivansh Rai Bacchan shahb.

Having an impressive start, we continued to chat. We slept @ 5 am in our respective places with a promise to meet for the celebration soon.

I got up early to get fresh rose flower petals from the local florist, packed all the cards made for her and hit the street @ 8.30am.

After reaching to her area, I parked the car near the mosque and arranged all the rose petals on the sun visor of the passenger seat, adjusted the sun visor on driver side with selfie stick stuck between the two sun visors.

As she entered the car and sat on passenger seat, looked at me with questionable view in her still sleepy eyes, I leaned to kiss her eyes, said "Happy Birthday", played song by Rafi "*Baharon phool barsao......*" my other hand turned the sun visors and viola, all rose petals fell over her.

She was dumb stuck for may minutes appreciating the flowers, now her looks changed to a lover's looks and she hugged me.

"This is the best gift on my birthday I have ever received."

"Wait, for more. Try to find more in the car itself."

Listening to this she started looking for treasure hunt like a child.

She found a soft toy in the glove box, many small cards underneath the seat and lots of chocolates in the rear pocket of the seat.

Seeing the child inside her come out to explore the gifts was a visual treat.

Reading the small cards her eyes became moist, she looked up, kissed me passionately and said, "What will happen to me when you will not be with me?

These gifts, cards, flowers and this moment is the most special for me.

I have never felt so much pampered in my life after I became an adult. Never leave me."

She leaned over my arm and started reading all the cards again.

When she had finished, I handed her a wrapped gift which initially she took for a diary and gave me a questioning look.

"Open it gently" I said.

The shinning wrapping paper was soon lying on the car mat and another golden shiny plaque was in front of her widely opened eyes.

The plague had the inscription "101 Attributes of Jyshri".

Starting from point number 1, as great kisser and ending to 101 as a pure soul, it was a decent description of her that she was unaware of.

She was now having tears of joy. Long moments passed, no one spoke, she kept looking at me with a look suggesting that these moments will be cherished for a very long time.

I stroked her hair and said, "I will always be with you, for you even when we will become old, I will keep caring for you the same way."

"Now go and get ready, as I told you another surprise is waiting for you. I will see you at the selected place by 12 noon. Try to come alone."

She kept her posture on my arm and said, "In you I have found everything

I have desired. You know it is not possible now for me to come alone.

I have to take Vikram as my alibi."

I knew this would happen, so it was better not to argue.

As is usual with the females, she got late in dressing up and came to my office exactly one hour late.

Not to mention, she was looking stunningly beautiful, below knee-length black

lace top with the same red overcoat, my favorite red lip color, curls on hair and

light blue eye liner made her look like a celebrity star.

Vikram was in casuals, not following the black dress code and was looking an odd man out.

I opened the passenger door for her and seated her, she felt like a queen.

Vikram settled on the rear seat.

We started for the venue with our chosen songs playing which we were enjoying secretly while Vikram was busy in his cell phone.

After one more hour of cruising through difficult traffic flow we reached The Lalit, where I had made arrangements sans the room as I was not in a mood for threesome which I have seen only in porn movies and have hated.

At the lobby level, musician with guitar & violin were waiting and, on my nod, started playing happy birthday song.

We settled for Indian restaurant on first floor, there was another surprise waiting for her in the form of a floral welcome by hotel staff as we alighted the elevators.

We took a corner table with full daylight falling on the furniture.

Jyshri asked me if we could change the restaurant as there were no other guests in this one.

I suggested that we can explore the other 2 restaurants near the lobby, Vikram conveyed that he would wait in the restaurant, she looked up to me and I had to accompany her.

We boarded the lift, although it was to descent one floor only, its slow pace gave her enough time to hug and kiss me and thanking me for the arrangements.

She was having wonderful time of her life.

We just strolled the restaurants for the sake of passing few minutes before we joined Vikram on the designated table.

The musicians were waiting for the celebration to start.

I reckoned the waitress to bring cake and the musicians to start.

The cake was made fresh at Azote as per her wish.

I brought out a silver-colored studded crown and placed it on her hair and we clapped on music while she cut the cake.

The musician asked us to sing along the chosen numbers and we enjoyed the flow.

I gave her more gifts, including a big size card, her photo calendar, a panda, a mug to drink etc. which she accepted with wide eyes.

Vikram gave her a pen and stated that he will give her a ring.

She looked at the left index finger and then towards my eyes indicating that her left ring finger is waiting for me.

We enjoyed the ethnic fine Indian cuisine.

A photo shoot followed it as usual for any party to capture memories.

In one of the snap, she stood beside the sofa on which I was sitting and gave a pose like we see a king sitting on throne and his queen keeping right elbow on the shoulder of king with left hand on her waist.

We came back with happy moments memories.

Chapter 10

Chest Pain

14.05.2008

It is about 7pm and I have finished counseling last patient of today about face aesthetics, when my secretary informed me about a lady who is requesting for an urgent consultation.

We doctors cannot refuse any patient even if the days schedule is over. In comes Jyshri, after sitting on the chair she informed that she has been experiencing pain in the left lower side of chest for past few days.

I take a detailed history and ask her to walk in the clinic to see if this is angina.

All is good with her, I asked her to see a physician as if the pain persists, it falls in the domain of a physician or cardiologist.

I told her that I do not keep an ECG machine. As a doctor I auscultated her and heart beats sound perfect. She took my finger and put it just lateral to the sternum bone where the margins of breasts start, she indicated that the pain starts from here and then took my palm to cover her breast.

"The pain subsides if the breast is pressed."

I withdraw my hand to laugh before prescribing a muscle relaxant.

"You should relax more; this is nothing but a muscular pain."

"I wish I could relax; my divorce decree is awaited, then I have a whole life with uncertain limits to explore. I am not sure where I will go or what I will do but..........."

"If you have some time, can I offload some thing from my mind? As I have no one to talk about this, everyone is busy in their own world, I chose this time Sir as I knew that you would be free by now."

Was it a request or demand I could not differentiate, I had no choice but to lend my ear for few minutes, while my staff did all the days closing work in background.

I nodded.

She took a long breath and acknowledged by thanking and started unfolding few pages of her life related to genital warts.

"I was happy to get married to Himanshu Agarwal, I had dreamt of a fairy tale life.

Soon I had given him good news of missing my periods, my in laws did not like it, my mom in law said that it was too soon to start a family and showed me dreams of enjoying early years of married life without children. I was carried away by her suggestions and despite confirmed pregnancy, I foolishly fell into her trap and got it terminated at a nearby nursing home in Paschim Vihar, I went to the nursing home wearing my *shaadi ka chooda* the doctor and staff were surprised.

After this episode all of them changed colors, they invited me to take alcohol in front of in laws, eat non vegetarian food and what not. Life was changing gears and my mother-in-law made me leave the house with my husband to stay in a rented accommodation, he had his own plans to continue with his girlfriends and going to massage parlors and Thailand for enjoyment. Later, I filed for divorce when he left me after having invited a call girl and his friends at our rented accommodation for fun and booze.

I was broken from all quarters, my husband had left me penny less, whatever I earned from my salary before marriage was spent in hiring a very slow lawyer.

One day I was wandering in the premises of Rohini court when I saw 2 young lawyers sitting on a shaded bench, I was feeling thirsty and I asked them for a water station, one of them was gracious enough to hand me a freshwater bottle. During our talks which followed, after I told them my story, the same lawyer said that they are doing an internship and will fight my case for no money. I felt relaxed and promised to hand over my case to him. During next few days on the pretext of understanding the whole case and signing documents, he asked me my current address and knocked on my door, I was happily surprised to see him as my messiah. I developed emotions for him and revealed the same to him, he said that he also liked me and will try to get the case solved quickly in my favor so that we can marry. This opened up a new world for me and then we started having regular intimate moments. Little did I know that he was already married and that he would give this infection. It was in the court premises that some other lawyer asked him about the health of his son and that gave me another shock.

I wanted to shout on him but did not dare to do so. It broke me further." She paused to take few sips of water.

"Now Sir, tell me where is the scope for me to relax? I am all alone, with diseases, no money, no one to talk to........thanks for giving me your time."

Before I could say anything, she got up and left the room hiding her eyes which by now became moist.

I called the receptionist to inform that this patient is to be given 50% discount in fee for today's consultation.

Chapter 11

Jaipur trip

"*Mujhe kahin le chalo, main bahut pareshan ho gai hu apni zindagi se.*"

Her response to my early morning hello on phone came as a jitter.

"*Kya hua.*"

"*Zindagi ki lag gai hai, maa mujhe jeene nahi deti, tum mujhe marne nahi dete ho,*

Vikram *ka koi bharosa nahi hai, main kya karoon?*"

"Both my sisters are well settled now in their life, my mom keeps good relations

with them and has a special love for my differently-abled deaf and dumb brother, but no one wants to look at me. When in problem they call me for help but when I need them, they are aliens to me."

"I want to go out for some time, Vikram is also busy with his sister's divorce, you are busy with your family and practice, what about me?"

"Please take me to some place or else I will do something unusual which will pain everyone."

I laughed and said "*Jo garajte hain wo baraste nahi hain*. Never mind, let's go to Jaipur,

I have a meeting there and will come next day by afternoon."

"No, I cannot go with you for a long time more than a day, if I am going with you then

I have to come back home by late evening, as you are married so it should not create problems and I should not be called home breaker."

Oh, so considerate about your own reputation, I thought.

"Ok, let's catch morning Shatabdi express, go there, freak out and return by evening

Shatabdi train, if that sounds Ok with you."

"Hmm.....tell me what will I say to Vikram? He will ask a thousand questions."

"You go with him to any place you want, leave me out of this." Was my dry reply.

"No you do not understand, no one knows about us, Vikram thinks that I have no life except to dance on to his tunes, I am trapped, you are a breath of fresh air with no strings attached with me, you know what I want........"

"Then what is Vikram doing among us? You are impossible to deal with." I snapped.

"Ok baba, I will come, do not worry about my problems, I want to get out of it, may be for a short time." She surrendered.

Next morning, we boarded Jaipur Shatabdi express train from New Delhi Railway station, she enjoyed the train journey as if she was travelling in train for the first time.

The train reached its destination on time; I had booked a room in a nearby five star hotel for day boarding only. It was a few minutes' walk after that we checked in the room.

"Can I order food as room service, as I am tired and do not want to go to restaurant?" She said hugging me to thank for the journey so far.

I nodded, looked into her eyes and said, "I am not in favor of wasting time before catching the return train. So let's enjoy our day out."

She helped me in removing each others clothes and we hit the shower together.

After a warm shower, we decided not to wear anything till out checkout time.

In between I ordered food and continued our cuddling while watching movies on room television.

A bell broke our rhythm, it was the room service guy.

I asked her to cover herself in white sheets and lay on bed, while I wore bathing gown loose enough to hide my excited member and opened the door.

The guy smiled, placed food on the table, debited the credit card, and left. It probably was a usual sight for him.

We could not resist the fragrance of food after a long journey, warm shower and cuddle act, our gut had become more demanding.

Eating naked, her sitting on my lap was a great experience. I dropped some sauce on my member and she understood to lick it and took me inside her mouth to make me hard.

During her return journey, she slept on my shoulder with relaxed features on her face.

Chapter 12

2016 Pseudo movie show

I receive a call from her that she wants to go for a movie with me today. I ask her to come to clinic during my lunch hour as I have a break in afternoon.

I booked 2 tickets online and was waiting for her.

She is not responding to my phone calls and comes late.

She is wearing a red dress, with high heels and deep red lipstick, kajal is looking great on her.

"Now it will be late for us to see the movie from beginning,

if you wish we can still grab our seats." I try to be calm.

"First I will grab some food as I am hungry and then we may

go for movie sometime later" she drops a bomb indicating that the

ticket prices have to be forgotten and now I have to arrange lunch for her.

"Why, what has happened today?"

"It is my younger sister and her husband are fighting to end their marriage and I was trying to patch them up, but I have left them to settle their barbs on their own, and have come here, please do something, I am hungry"

What option did I have?

She settled in for daal rice from Haldiram. By the time, her food was delivered, she asked me to check her lower back for a muscle pull.

I obliged and asked her to lay on patient examination bed, exposing her back, as I palpated (a method to observe clinically with palm), she said that she was feeling great and requested me to do the same maneuvers on the whole of her back. She allowed me to go under her bra straps and soon was emitting sounds of pleasure.

After some time, she got up and hugged me for pleasure. Her hands were shaking, and she lifted one of her thighs to wrap around my waist, it was a clear indication that she was ready for anything. She offered me her lips in return of the massage and never looked back.

A new movie with new characters was shown in person for the next 40 minutes.

Chapter 13

G I P Mall

25.07.2019

I am about to reach the clinic when Jyshri called to enquire about plans for the day.

"I have some patients lined up for consultation and may be some procedures, you want to join to learn anything?"

"I was thinking if you have the day for me, actually I have heard a lot about the

Great India Place mall at Noida, have you been there? It is a good place to hang out and do some shopping."

"I have never been there" I responded.

"Oh, great we can explore the same together, can you take out time today?" came reply or a request I could not make out.

"I cannot say, anyways we have to search for the property you are looking for and

I have kept few hours after lunch for the same" I spoke, reminding her about the 2-room the floor she wants to purchase near her mom's house but in her own name and without her funds, if any.

"I know floor is important, we can discuss about it during our way to the mall, please make it possible today, my mom has gone to my sister's place, and I have no one to ask me where I am going today."

"Oh, that is a great opportunity, I can come over and we will have a good time. You can make biryani and then we will go floor hunting for you." I offered to save me from driving all the way to Noida.

"No chance mister, my neighbors are neither deaf or blind, moreover you have never come here so more eyebrows will be raised.

I will invite you to my new home when we purchase the floor, you can come for lunch" she played a defensive stroke.

"Why on lunch, why not for dinner?" I demanded.

"Look you will come as a guest and the guests do not stay for long time, also Vikram will be staying with me so…."

"What??? What did you just say, Vikram will stay with you?

Why on earth am I a fool to invest rupees fifty lakhs and you will have a live in partnership with Vikram? Are you kidding?" My anger was more palpable.

"Oh come on Jaan, I was really joking, now pick me up from our usual meeting point and we will have the full day, *aaoge na*?"

Reluctantly I agreed to her plan and parked my car in front of the DDA Flats where a florist has shop and waited trying to analyze what she has just said.

After full 15 minutes of waiting, I saw her coming towards the car, wearing a blue top on xpose brand jeans pair and with same signature black hand bag cum purse. Smile is the most dangerous weapon females have when they know that there is something wrong done on their part, I am no exception that it kills all your anger, emotions etc. etc.

"Hi" she sat on the passenger seat and smiled, took my hand into hers and squeezed.

"*Chalo na mood kyo kharab hai.*"

"*Tune hi kiya haiab theek bhi tu hi karegi.*" I snapped.

"Ok if you do not want to go with me, I will not force you." Came a googly.

"Look I have already cancelled all my patient appointments and now please do not irritate me anymore." I started the engine and drove towards Noida.

On the way to mall, she kept on cracking jokes, talking about her clothes and neighbors but kept the topic away from Vikram.

Suddenly her phone started ringing and her face became pale, for a few seconds she froze, she showed me the name flashing.

It was Vikram.

She opened the window and requested me to slow down and drive alongside an autorickshaw.

"Hello,...... *haan main Ruhi ke ghar jaa rahi hoon, auto me hoon........ theek hai.*"

The window was closed after these words.

"I have told him that I am visiting Ruhi and will take an auto as he is busy framing some business program and this is why I asked you to go near an auto."

Smart girl, I thought, but a foolish one as one day she will get caught. At the GIP Mall she did not buy anything for herself instead, bought four Raymond's full sleeve shirts for me. Till evening we strolled the mall, holding hands and sometimes hugging each other. She gulped down three Heniken strong beer cans.

I was surprised at the sudden carefree behavior.

While we were returning towards her home, she started narrating the hardship she is facing at her mother's place and requested me to get her a floor where she will stay as a free soul.

"Ok, I will buy you one floor, but if you will allow me to see you at my free will." I said as I wanted her to be clear in what she wants albeit under the effect of beer.

"This will not be possible as I would like to have the floor registered in my sole name and I will then decide about other things, I will then ask Vikram to stay with me, leaving his family and will make him agree on anything which I want."

"What……. Again Vikram, if you want the property in your name and want him to be your live-in partner, ask him to do the needful of searching the property and funding it, keep me out of it. I am not a fool to pay for him to enjoy life with you."

I spoke sternly and wanted to drop her at the earliest after knowing her plans.

"Vikram does not have money, why can't you buy me a floor, you have the money, you love me, I sleep with you, I come with you always, and now you are refusing to pay for my property." She demanded.

"Any sensible person will not do this for you or anybody. You do not have money and if you suddenly purchase a floor for rupees fifty lakhs, I am sure your family members and others who know you will ask questions. Never mind, I have a sense that you are doing this as you want only property from me."

"See, my uncle offered me to be his keep and was ready to give me property, but I did not budge, because I wanted you."

"But you want Vikram." I interrupted.

"I have no other choice, and I have to take back my eight years which I have spent listening to his orders, now I want to give orders. Table will turn and he will run after me, you only can make this possible, and I love you so please do it for me."

"I am not able to understand your math. I will talk about this later, but if I am purchasing any property, it will bear my name, you can be a joint owner." I dropped her at the same place near her home and drove towards mine.

It was a shocking revelation made by her and I felt dejected only for money by a gold digger all these years.

The next day, she did not call me, neither I tried calling her.

Few days passed and finally I went to her office.

Both of them were eating lunch, neither offered me anything including a seat.

I understood that.

"Jyshri, can you please give me back my Citibank credit card."

My words fell like a bomb on her, and as a thunderous surprise to Vikram.

In a feeble, stammering voice, she said she was not carrying it and would get it later.

Next day evening, while returning from a hospital after seeing an admitted patient,

I received a call from Vikram enquiring about the credit card @ 10.35pm.

Very few times he has called me.

“Can we talk while you probably are driving? Why have you given her the credit card?”

He wanted to know.

“You must know the role of credit card, it to purchase anything.” I replied diplomatically.

“Yes, but she does not need it, I do not understand the purpose?”

“Who does not need free money to spend? It is late and I think that you are mature enough to understand whatever you are asking. For anything more you can ask her.”

I wanted to cut the call short.

“I am highly confused as to why you have given your money to her to spend, I am fulfilling her needs, she has been avoiding the topic of discussion about your credit card, she has it as I have seen now.

I want to hear from you as to why have you given access to your financial instruments to her, you are just a friend.” He wanted to know more.

Poor Vikram could not have imagined the whole story.

Although, I used to suspect that he has an idea, but hats off to Jyshri, she has kept the things under wrap, so far.

"Maybe she will tell you better about her needs and by the way I never said about what she is doing with my credit card, sleep off, it is late."

I disconnected the phone.

He called again for the same reason, I politely declined to discuss stating that it is a personal matter.

Chapter 14

Sara Kuan

In past some years our relationship is not as smooth as it was, her expectations are different as she wants the same thing with me, to offer herself for comforts, I keep pressing her to settle in her life and marry someone except Vikram, I will support her.

I even offered to play role of *ladkiwala*. She always laughs at this thought. One evening she had a fight with her mother and was upset, she called me during my evening hospital rounds and asked for the name of a tranquilizer pill which I sent her as text.

After nearly one hour she told me she was feeling ok and going to sleep. In the mid of night @ 3 am I received a text that she was finding it difficult to sleep and wanted to talk,

I saw the message in the morning.

I tried calling her, she did not pick up.

"How are you feeling now?" I wrote as message.

After nearly two hours, she called me.

"Why do you send messages? My whole family was gathered today to discuss something, someone could have seen the same. Also, when I am not responding to call, please wait for my response." She was not in her usual avatar.

"Ok I will send you a message which only you will be able to understand, I will write SARA KUAN."

"What does that mean?"

"Translate it in English and it becomes ALL WELL. If you answer in Y,

I will wait for the call or else will call sooner."

"OK baba, do what you like." She surrendered.

"There is a new movie named *De De Pyaar De*. I want to see that after so much of tension. Will you be with me?" she spoke.

"Yes I will be, let me check on bookmy show."

I checked and we settled for 12noon show at Tilak Nagar Waves cinema.

After the movie she was feeling better, we ate some fast food and

then she asked me to buy some jewelry and change her spectacles for her.

We searched at Tanishq Paschim Vihar, Pitampura and Malabar and she settled for four diamond rings, one necklace and a mang tika.

She requested me slide one of the rings of her choice into her ring finger and, with moist eyes thanked me.

I was dearer by a few lakh rupees.

The Titan eye plus at Rohini was our next destination for her choice of frame.

It was still late afternoon when she remembered that she has to buy slippers and some suits.

Rajouri garden market came to her rescue as I had no other idea.

A shop called Indigo had a mannequin wearing sparkling knee length dress which caught her eye and soon was in her bag after trial.

Five suits from Delhi wala shop and few footwears form Stelatoes were sufficient for today's shopping.

Before reaching to the spot near her home she asked me to have coffee at CCD Rohini.

I was surprised as why she was spending so much time and money.

While alighting, she thanked me and said that all these she had dreamt of to do with me as a couple and now she has done it.

Little did I realize that SARA KUAN meant all gone into the well.

Chapter 15

Curses on the Soul

First is the lack of a stable relationship. Having a strained relationship with family members especially mother has tormented her beliefs in getting along with anyone, she has been running away from people whenever someone has tried to be nice to her. She has been having affairs with many men including her husband Himanshu, Vikram, her lawyer, a cardiologist, myself and more.

This lack of a stable relationship has forced her into a divorce, poverty, dependence upon others for a place to stay, eat and even talk to.

The trivial stabilizing feature is there in choosing her career too! She has jumped jobs from being a receptionist, to a manager, to an accountant, to a beautician, to marketing executive, a call center executive, fortune teller, assistant in petty projects but have never stayed at one place.

Further adding to financial woes and desperate to have someone she has taken the route of luring males and have extracted money to satisfy her taste of bespoke lifestyle.

The ongoing problem is age, as her age is advancing, due to lack of proper three meals and a healthy relationship, she has started showing wrinkles on the face, falls sick frequently most of the times with an upset belly, missing menstrual cycles for months (not due to pregnancy), urine infections (due to intimate relations) and nasal congestion, a permanent dental problem has never left her.

As with all humans, medical ailments keep pulling her legs.

Hell broke loose during 2020 when an unknown, unseen virus stared spreading from humans to humans by way of respiratory route - Covid 19, the mankind suddenly started feeling the importance of face masks, she was desperate to get mask of her small face size. As a fanatic cleanser, she tried her level best to keep pace with sanitization drive as recommended by our government and various medical agencies including WHO. All this proved to be of little help.

Then she contracted Covid 19!

Covid 19 infection made a paradigm shift in her life. Her boyfriend Vikram gave her this dreaded virus of the century as an infection.

This is not new for her and has been a case with all previous medical problems where she has found herself facing the fence alone after getting infections due to sexual relations.

Each episode of such infection since 2005 has taken a toll and has intensified. This one broke her to the bone.

She was all alone, gasping for breath, fighting fever, not knowing if she will see the light of tomorrow.

All public facilities were closed, no help was available, fortunately money transactions were happening without getting close and that was some respite.

Her immune system started crying for help. Fear of infection prevented her from taking any medical help as it would need her to walk into a hospital or clinic.

Previous prescription medicines were not helpful, and the fever spiked to 103.7 F.

She was lying on her bed, helpless but not ready to succumb.

Her mother sensed the gravity of the situation and shifted her down to her floor to take care.

Gradually she became dependent on her caregiver.

Four months have passed since she has recovered from the fever and weakness but is not able to breathe as she used to earlier. Walking was not a task earlier but now after Covid, it seems to be taxing exercise, like a pupil feels for sudden announcement of homework just after school breaks are intimated.

Very often a nebulizer session has become necessity.

Her immune system has attracted Covid -19 three times during all the waves of Covid.

Her mom's home was put under Red Zone and a police surveillance was assigned outside the lane during the 1st wave.

Being small face, dentists too have had tough times treating with root canal treatments. She has visited different dentists with different male accomplices who were looked upon for payment and they obliged remembering the close moments passed with her and in hope for future good times with her.

Being myopic has always hindered her to visualize her partners expressions during love making, and hence she has always gone for an expensive prescription glass and top of the order spectacle frames, since the bill was footed to the male partner.

Her taste for a good life is commendable. Five-star restaurant meals, never using public transport as she chooses a boyfriend who has a good car, at least a respectable hatchback.

She persuaded Vikram to change from a motorbike to car in 2007 when they started dating.

We have discussed these problems often and I have come to a solution which involves marriage. She has religiously been avoiding the topic of marriage as with one family, there will be restrictions in spending, outing, shopping and when she cannot make food for herself, it is a foolish thought to expect her to do so for a family.

Despite all this and staying hungry for many days, she understands the meaning of hunger. Whenever she is out on lunch with anyone, she never misses an opportunity to feed hungry beggars on the street. This gives her mental satisfaction.

There is a common solution to all three problems of her life and she knowingly avoids the talk of marriage. Her relatives, friends and well-wishers have now stopped mentioning the same for her.

She has explored the same solution once against all her family members especially her mother, but has failed miserably, now she is not ready to take a plunge again.

Doodh ka jala chaach bhi phoonk phoonk ke peeta hai. Instead, she has been testing waters with many different male partners, all of them having a family.

She has destroyed few families as if she is taking revenge from all married men for her life's ordeal.

Maybe she is suffering for some reason known to her.

She has had a difficult childhood, as she has narrated, very difficult adolescent and cursed adulthood. Her dealing with life is tilted away from the ordinary. Solo staying with sleeping naked is not an unusual act but frequently dreaming about having sex with her father and then the old man dying during the act because of a heart attack was not normal.

During one of her interviews, she said that she has a childhood female friend who is married at Rajouri Garden and whenever she visits her, both sleep together for a few hours in the afternoon as lesbians satisfying their needs.

Getting intimidated by the word of a family/marriage/ in laws has become her usual routine. Search for a stable relationship with no strings attached but loads of money to spend is now the goal of her life.

Her boyfriend's words "*dil kisi ko mat dena chahe jism kitno ko de dena*" has made a permanent engraving on her conscious and unconscious self.

It has led to the disastrous life she has thrown herself into. Her life is cursed if someone looks from outside and, the only solution is a stable relationship in terms of marriage.

From her eyes, life with all freebies, sex, booze sans a husband and in-laws is what she can live on.

Chapter 16

I am THAT I am

It has been more than four years since I have heard from her side or from any of her known person.

Her sister called me up this year on my birthday and opened a new avenue.

"Sir, a very happy birthday! I hope that you are doing well in the life."

"Thanks for the wishes Ruhi, how are you? How is auntyji and after so many years of silence, I am surprised to hear your voice.

Is everything alright?" I replied.

"Yes Sir, all is good except that Jyshri didi is not with us."

This sentence was cold as cold as it could get.

"Oh, so finally she got settled in her life, good for her." I said being optimistic about her.

"Sir, I think that you are unaware that she left the house some years ago and is not traceable.."

"What?" I interrupted, "you guys never told me earlier and you are telling me this after so long oh God, why?"

After a pause came the reply.

"She never wanted you to know, she gave us written instructions which we found after she was gone, she said that if you came to know about all this, she will end her life."

Her voice started shaking.

"How about Vikram? Does he know? I am sure that he is supporting auntyji."

Again, a long pause.

"Vikram bhaiya was the catalyst for her taking this decision.

She left immediately after he expired." The words now started giving me chills.

This was like a movie scene.

"How, what happened?" I could utter these words only, in disbelief.

"He had a heart attack and could not be saved, that broke my sis and she left the city probably to become a saint. She left a note saying that you should not be told anything about all this and has left a small, sealed packet to be delivered to you today, on your birthday."

She tried to give details in a few words.

"Is your clinic at the same place as earlier? I will send the packet via a delivery app and it will reach to you in no time." She asked.

"Yes, I am at the same place, but I would like to know more about all this."

"Sir, I think answers to all your questions will be found in the packet, as we have found ours.

The information I have given is the only one any of us will tell you.

We have tried to find her everywhere but in vain, she is alive we know as we all receive gifts during our important days. This is all I can tell you as of now. I am sending the packet bearing your name and today's date as written by didi, please accept it." She then excused disconnecting the call.

I waited to receive the consignment with mixed feelings, the whole 17 years of events started opening up layer by layer within me and I was feeling to have lost some one very near to me.

Finally, the packet was in my hands, I opened it carefully, as informed my name and today's date was written with a ball pen on a paper pasted on the cardboard box wrapped in plastic tapes.

It took me a few minutes to carefully unwrap the tapes and to open the pandora's box. There I found various memoirs and a note written on plain paper,

"Happy Birthday, by now you must have come to understand why

I have never contacted you. I knew that if you came to know about my disappearance, you would have left no stone unturned to find me. But now I am far from all of you, and I am safe, happier and freer from all strings, I can say that I have found solace for which I was searching, now I do not have to take anybody's support and I am not answerable to anyone. Do not think that I am involved with anyone, you are the one and only in my life and I assure you all that I am not doing anything wrong to be ashamed of. You used to say '*time kam hai*' and I never realized that my time to find myself and the eternal peace is limited. I promise to meet you one day when the time will come and die in your arms if God permits. You can find the articles which you showered upon me with so many emotions except one ring which I consider the link of the past seventeen years in this birth and all our previous births and I am wearing it till my departure from this world.

Please be happy, do not try to look for me as it will be a useless exercise. As promised, I will meet you some day. Till we meet - SARA KUAN!!!"

Dedicated to my beloved wife and two beautiful children who have missed me while writing this book.